SURPRISE ATTACK!

SURPRISE ATTACK!

by John Clagett

JULIAN MESSNER · NEW YORK

PUBLISHED SIMULTANEOUSLY IN THE UNITED STATES AND CANADA BY
JULIAN MESSNER, A DIVISION OF SIMON & SCHUSTER, INC.,
1 WEST 39 STREET, NEW YORK, N.Y. 10018. ALL RIGHTS RESERVED.

PRINTED IN THE UNITED STATES OF AMERICA
LIBRARY OF CONGRESS CATALOG CARD NO. LC 68-17522

1440618

CONTENTS

CONTENTS

SURPRISE ATTACK!

ONE

THE LAUNCHING

"I NEVER WOULD HAVE believed it," Jerry O'Donnell said, running the wooden spoon around the now empty paper cup, "but I'll be a little sorry to leave here tomorrow." The August day was warm and sunny, and the five young men sat at one of the outdoor tables at the ship's service store. Green lawns began beyond the gray buildings, and continued up a gentle hill to the right to the first barracks. Beyond the barracks Jerry could see the black bulk of the old frigate *Constellation,* with the admiral's flag flying from her mainmast. Narragansett Bay glinted in the sunlight, and a few sea gulls were drifting in the wind.

"Did you hear that, Tom?" Clay Harkness drawled, his light blue eyes twinkling. "Our Boston Irishman actually saying he liked Naval Training Station, Newport? Boot camp?" He reached down and rubbed the stiff canvas leggings that enclosed the dungarees about his calves, the leggings that symbolized his status as seaman recruit, or boot.

"That's because a pint of ice cream has just slid under that pug nose. He'll get hungry again in a minute and change his mind." Tom Bellido looked into his own cup and sighed to find it empty. He shrugged his heavy shoulders and then grinned.

"Also, we graduate tomorrow," Larry White added. "I never thought the day would come!"

"I didn't say I really liked the joint," Jerry protested. "But I guess we've done pretty well here, all of us."

The civilian at the soda fountain leaned over to the red-faced Chief Petty Officer in his sharp khakis.

"Looks funny to see those five boots sitting there during working hours, Chief," he said, idly. "How come?"

The CPO turned to look at the five young men.

"Those are the platoon commanders of the color company. I reckon they've earned the right to take it easy for a few minutes. They're good boys." He grinned and turned back to his coffee.

"I think," Einar Andersen said at the table, "that my eyes have gone funny. I swear I saw Bull McGee smile at us."

"You ate your ice cream too fast," Jerry said. "It went to your head. Bull McGee smile? He don't know how."

Jerry heard the others laugh at his words, but he didn't join them. He had a funny, sick sensation inside. Maybe the others didn't feel any suspense, but he was full of it. Graduation tomorrow, and this afternoon orders would be posted. He had fought against waiting until he was through high school to enlist, but his father had stood firm. Jerry had been afraid that the war would be over before he could get into it. Now, with basic training almost over, he was a lot older, somehow, and a lot smarter. He'd been to the station hospital; he'd seen the guys with arms or legs gone. All the chief petty officers at the boot camp had seen action, plenty of it, and movies, lectures and bull sessions had shown Jerry what the war was really like. And he knew, in this August of 1943, that it was a long way from being over.

He looked around at the others, not hearing for the moment their idle talk. It was strange to him that a couple of months before he had never met any of them. Now they seemed like his oldest and best friends.

Clay Harkness was the first Rebel he'd ever known—well, half a Rebel. Kentucky wasn't considered the real, deep South. Clay was short and slim, with brown hair and blue eyes, friendly and easy; but he had a temper. He and Tom Bellido had started out like two tomcats on a back fence. Clay had even tried to take on the wide, tough Italian boy one Sunday in barracks, but Tom had just grinned, wrapped his long arms around Clay and hung on. In a minute Clay had started to laugh, and the two had been friends ever since.

Like Jerry, Larry White was looking thoughtful. He was

medium size, with a twang to his voice and muscles well developed by farm work. Larry was from Vermont, an apple knocker, and he had a lot of good stories about deer hunting, what he called pattridge and the Green Mountains.

Then there was Einar Andersen. What a guy. Six feet tall— not heavy, but solid. He was even stronger than Tom, but nobody had ever seen him use his strength against another man and he'd give a shipmate his last dime. His eyes were deep blue, and his fair skin had been burned permanently bronze working on his father's fishing boat in Seattle. Looking at Einar made Jerry feel better.

Jerry found Einar looking at him; he grinned, and the Norwegian winked.

Einar Andersen thought: Wish I could be like O'Donnell. Look at him—not worrying about a thing. Orders coming up, and he doesn't care. Me, I'm scared. Maybe I'll get that destroyer I asked for, and the destroyers are right in the middle of it. The Chief says a lot of us will go right out to the Pacific as replacements. What happened to the guys we'll replace?

Clay Harkness looked at the grinning Jerry. If these Yankees don't worry about where they're going, he thought, darned if I will either. Anyway, there'll be two weeks leave starting after graduation, and I can get home again. Spoon bread and country ham. His mouth watered. Then he thought again about the orders, and his smile faded. He opened his mouth to say something, and was stopped by the sight of a boy running toward them.

"Einar, Einar!" the boy shouted, grinning widely. "They're posted! You're going to a destroyer!"

Einar froze, then felt a hot rush of gladness. The fear was gone, at least for now. A destroyer, the seaman's ship! He'd got his pick, he had his job!

"Thanks, Joe," he said. "A destroyer, huh?"

Joe's reply was drowned as the four other young men broke from their momentary paralysis and began a rush toward the bulletin board outside Administration. They found a surging crowd before it, and only gradually could they work their way in to stand before the long list.

Tom Bellido found his name near the top. For a moment the letters blurred and shifted before his eyes, then cleared. Gunnery school! He had put in for it; he had known that with his record at boot camp, especially on the marksmanship range and at gun drill, he had had a good chance. Gunnery school. He felt a wild exultation, but then a small voice within him said: And you won't have to go to sea for two or three months! Safe that much longer! And he felt ashamed and backed away, out of the excited throng.

Jerry O'Donnell stood before the board, fists clinched. Motor Torpedo Boat School, Melville, Rhode Island. PT boats! Since he had first seen the sleek, fast boats in the newsreels he had hoped for this. He had heard that the PT boys were plenty tough, that that was what the initials stood for.

Clay Morehead Harkness—Submarine School, New London. Clay felt the sweat roll down his ribs, gather slightly on his forehead. He had it, he had it! Did he want it? Submarines!

Sub school, dives, practice with Momsen lungs in the escape tower, steel tanks, compression. Could he take it? He'd always felt uneasy when pinned into a place, or a situation, with no easy way out. Could he take this now?

He would. He swore he would.

Larry White was assigned to Radio School. Fine. He liked code, its meaningful buzzing and clicking; he liked the smell of electricity and hot metal and glass. And he felt wings growing within him. He had his course laid out: get to be a good radioman, put in for flight duty as radioman-gunner on a carrier plane, get in a tour of duty and then try for flight school. After the war he would return to Vermont, become a crop-duster and fly a taxi and rental service. He would fly high above those Green Mountains he loved, and see them as the birds saw them.

The four young men drew together away from the crowd. They looked at each other with sober solemnity, then their smiles broadened. They rejoined Einar at the table he had held for them, and their smiles became laughs, then shouts and a wrestling, noisy celebration upon which Bull McGee directed a lenient and approving eye. They were getting good kids in the Navy now, and these five were tops.

The Chief's smile wavered a little, and his face became sad. He thought of his boy, out with Halsey. He hoped that he and these five fellows would get through the war all right. But he knew in his heart that when it was over, this particular group of five young men would not be complete. He had seen their requests and their assignments; they were going to the fighting jobs.

McGee had ridden the *Astoria* down at the Battle of Savo, and that had been plenty for him. But he'd be going back; he couldn't keep sending kids like these out to the war zone and not return there himself. Six months more, and he would work the transfer. Feeling sad, he turned away from the noisy crowd around the bulletin board and headed for the CPO Club, which would now be open.

The ship's service store was crowded, and the air of celebration was intense. Perhaps for most it covered a considerable uneasiness about the war that lay before them; if so, it was well covered. Except for the sameness of the dress—dungaree shirts and pants, leggings and white hats—the young men could have been the members of a high school or prep school celebrating some sporting victory, or perhaps the end of exams.

Jerry O'Donnell said, "I think I'll go buy a big, thick cigar. This is a special occasion."

"Ayuh," agreed Larry White. "Then you can get seasick even before you get on a ship."

"The Boston Mick?" queried Tom Bellido. "Why, man, they wean those boys on chewing tobacco."

"That's right, I forgot. And they cut their teeth on ice skates, huh, Jerry?"

"Better than boiling sap to syrup and twisting cow's tails."

"You mean *caows,* don't you?" asked Clay Harkness, grinning. "Don't confuse the old Vermonter."

Tom Bellido noticed that Einar was looking a little sad; this was unusual, for the big second-generation Norwegian was usually serene and undisturbed.

"What's the matter, Einar?" he said quietly. "Anything wrong?"

Einar's answer came at a lull in the talk, so that the other four heard what he said.

"I was just thinking," Einar said, "that it has been fun being with you four fellows. I was thinking that we will be together the rest of today and tomorrow morning, and then tomorrow afternoon we will all leave for different places. I wonder if we will ever be together again?"

The silence grew as the five boys looked at each other, thinking hard.

"Yes," Larry said. "That's right." He was silent again, for a moment. "A year from now—I wonder where we'll be a year from now, and how far apart. A year from now. . . ."

TWO

OPENING MOVES

THE YEAR PASSED, and a little more. The five young men who had eaten ice cream together on that August day still survived, veterans now and all at sea. They had changed greatly. The war too had changed, and on this October 23, 1944, they were drawing together again, converging on the island of Leyte in the Philippines, not too far from a great bay called Leyte Gulf.

The American sea offensive against Japan was moving to its roaring climax. The Navy knew now that it would win, but it also knew that terrible months still lay ahead. Japanese naval air power was nearly destroyed, its latest reinforcements wiped out in the continuing strikes by Halsey and Task Force 38 against Okinawa and Formosa. The experienced enemy pilots had died during the Battle of the Philippine Sea; their replacements now were gone, and Japan would have a hard time replacing them. The schedule for the invasion of the Philippines was speeded up, and it was decided to hit the major island of Leyte instead of Mindoro, much farther south. A vast American fleet landed the army on Leyte on October 20. MacArthur went ashore with his men, and the Japanese high command resolved to throw all its remaining naval strength into a counterattack.

This strength was still formidable—four carriers, nine battleships, fourteen heavy cruisers, six light cruisers and thirty-five destroyers, the whole manned by fifty or sixty thousand well-trained officers and men. The Japanese fleet was very weak in air power; only a few planes with inexperienced crews were aboard the four carriers, and the land-based planes available were also flown by green pilots.

The American forces were vastly superior. Task Force 38 alone greatly outgunned the entire Japanese force, and there was a formidable fire support and bombardment group at Leyte Gulf and a covering force of eighteen escort carriers, with destroyer escorts, to furnish air support for the landings ashore.

But the area to be covered was great; this force was spread out, and the enemy had one logical and vulnerable target—the vast supporting and transport fleet in Leyte Gulf. If he could smash through to the great bay, a terrible defeat could be inflicted on the invading Americans.

The American commanders knew this. As the soldiers ground through the opposition ashore, planes and ships scouted for the first appearance of enemy warships.

The wide scouting net included American submarines, quiet, invisible, deadly.

Clay Harkness, lookout, stood on the dark, windswept starboard side bridge of the submarine *Darter,* resting his elbows on the spray shield, keeping the seven-fifty night glasses to his eyes. Ceaselessly he swept the glasses back and forth through his sector. A feeling of impending action filled the crowded bridge, although no light appeared except for a faint glow from the compass binnacle and an even fainter red light showing through the open hatch.

Each time Clay saw the dark blot that represented their patrol mate, the *Dace,* he had to repress an impulse to give the lookout's warning cry. Though she startled him, it was good to have her there, the only hope in case of serious trouble. These were enemy seas, island-studded, reef-slashed, dangerous.

Clay heard the talker's low-voiced report to Commander McClintock, the skipper. "Radar Plot reports contact, many surface ships, Captain."

"Tell him I'm coming down," the skipper said, and disappeared down the hatch. A new alertness came over the bridge. If major enemy forces were about, it was quite possible that a destroyer might be closing on them now, its radar echo jammed by reef, island or wave.

It seemed a long time before McClintock came back to the bridge. Even before he did so, Clay felt the decks begin to vibrate to a quicker rhythm as the submarine surged ahead through the night at top speed.

"Looks like a fleet, boys," McClintock announced when he returned. "Dead ahead, ten miles off. They're moving fast, though. Hope we can catch them."

The skipper hailed the *Dace* by megaphone and gave her the word; then, fifty yards apart, the two submarines tore along at their best speed. "Feel the old girl go!" Clay muttered to himself. At this high speed, the craft sawed up and down with a gentle hammocky motion; fine spray drifted back from the bows. When the bow dug under one of the small waves, green phosphorescence showed, and a long, pale-green track was unrolled aft. Clay hoped there were no planes about, but he knew that the phosphorescence couldn't be helped if they were going to catch the target fleet. Waves rolled aft along the hull, the diesel exhausts muttered, then fell silent as the water surged over them, then muttered again.

"Ask Radar Plot what target speed is now," McClintock ordered the talker. The man spoke into his phone mouthpiece; in a moment the answer came.

"Slowing down, Skipper. Latest estimate, fifteen knots."

"Good! We've got them now."

Even though it wasn't Clay's first action, he could feel his stomach tighten. But there was, as yet, nothing to do but wait. And watch! he reminded himself, his eyes and glasses still automatically covering his sector. Whatever happens ahead,

20

keep your eyes skinned on your job. Everybody's life, not to mention your own, could depend on your not missing anything that might become visible—wave on rock, fleck of bow wake, plane exhaust, mast against the dark sky.

Submariners were always conscious of the loneliness of their job. Usually their ships were quite alone on patrol; Clay was happy that it was not so now. Submarines died alone, usually, and in an environment and manner that left all their crew dead. But the *Dace,* that steel-enclosed cigar of space poised at the surface of the water and roaring through it at twenty knots, offered help, support and cheer.

In the meantime, Clay knew, the *Darter* must get well ahead of the enemy formation for a periscope attack at dawn. A contact report had been sent. It was imperative that definite information about the size and make-up of the enemy force be forwarded to the American admirals. It was known that the Japanese fleet was out, and it was believed that its target would be the invasion force at Leyte Gulf. But where would it assemble? What channel between islands would it use as an approach?

Clay knew that such information was considered to be more valuable than the continued life of the *Darter.*

The time dragged slowly by. Clay's eyes were tired of straining through the night; his knees and legs ached, and he was growing cold. The navigator came up from the conning tower. "Dave," he said, "we're ten miles ahead of them now, off the port bow of the formation. Plenty of ships—two columns. No scouting ships in front of the main body."

"Good! I'll slow to target speed, and we'll maintain this position. Tell Radar Plot to keep those ranges and bearings coming up."

Five minutes later, McClintock turned to the executive officer and said quietly: "Twenty minutes for coffee. See that every man aboard gets a cup."

"I can use a shot of mud myself," the Exec said, and then he dodged below.

When the coffee came it was steaming hot, and the heavy mug felt warm and comforting in Clay's hand. He drank, and the coffee warmed him through and made his stomach feel better. Coffee, he thought. What would the navy do without it?

Even as he drank, he kept his eyes on the sea and the sky. Death could come to the submarine from the sky between breaths, in spite of radar search, for the radar had been known to miss a plane's approach.

At 0450, the battle alarm sounded, quietly and without the klaxon that warns of a dive. Submariners are quiet people at sea, and there was little noise or confusion to mark the shift to complete battle readiness. The *Dace* turned away and disappeared into the darkness. She would cross the enemy column to attack from the starboard side.

At the sound of the general quarters alarm, Clay shivered with excitement; these last few minutes would be long and full of suspense. They were nearly dead ahead of a major enemy fleet; surely there must be some destroyers, aircraft, something, scouting ahead. If so, they would be sighted on his lookout sector. Why, oh why, does the skipper hang on? he asked himself. Why not go down where it's nice and quiet and nobody can see us?

It was five in the morning. There was a touch of gray in the east; dawn would come very soon. Clay heard the skipper's voice give crisp, quiet orders; then he felt the boat heel beneath him as she began a 180° turn, reversing course to run down the throat of the port column of enemy ships. Minutes now, Clay knew, but he kept his eyes on his search sector. He thought he could see a little farther, that the small whitecaps were more distinct. Good Lord, almost day—wasn't the skipper ever going to take her down? Clay was cold, he was scared and he was everlastingly eager for this attack to succeed. If the *Darter* were sighted. . . .

Ahoogah! Ahoogah! Ahoogah!

Every step known, every movement practiced, Clay was unsnapping the search glasses, searching for loose gear, moving across the deck with the other figures on the crowded bridge. Clay followed the man descending through the hatch. He looked up to see the skipper right behind him, standing for one moment on the ladder, head out of the hatch, looking. Then the hatchway came down with a clang, locked shut by the captain himself. The first lip of an engulfing wave washed through the edges of the hatch just before it was locked. A fast, silent dive! Clay grinned to himself. Without hesitation, he crossed the well-lighted, crowded conning tower and took the headphone set from a hook. He put it on and in a moment was in contact with forward and after torpedo rooms, battery room and engine room. He reported his battle circuit ready,

23

one report among a dozen others, then joined the silence that fell over the tower.

The deck was still inclined downward; the boat would go below periscope depth, trim and rise slowly again. Always there was the uneasy moment when a man wondered if there would be some mistake—if one man's error would send her on down, positive buoyancy unrecovered, driven into the depths below by her engines and her weight. Clay felt the uneasiness only momentarily. In the control room beneath, the diving officer, Ensign Bill Paseler, and Chief Strother were at the diving planes—no problem.

The *Darter* leveled and trimmed at three hundred feet, then moved slowly and steadily up to periscope depth. The scope whined in the well, with McClintock seizing the handles as they rose. In the silence, the conning tower team heard the skipper gasp. This startled them all, for McClintock was a calm man.

"What's there?" asked the Exec, Mr. Schwab.

"Battleships." McClintock swung the periscope a little farther and stopped.

"What's there?" asked the Exec hoarsely.

"Cruisers." The periscope was swung again, and again came the question and the answer. "Battleships and destroyers."

"My God," exclaimed the Exec, prayerfully. "It must be the whole Jap fleet!"

"And I'm looking right down the column," the skipper said. "Here, Ernie, take a quick look."

Schwab stepped in eagerly, and Clay could see the muscles

of his jaw and neck tense as he looked into the instrument. He stepped away with a strange smile on his face.

"Looks like Navy Day," he said. Clay felt an exasperated longing to take a look himself. He pushed the thought away and continued his low-voiced comments to the eagerly listening torpedo and engine room personnel.

At 0525 the first target was identified as a heavy cruiser making high speed. At 0527 all tubes were ready for firing, and the range was only three thousand yards. Just then the enemy column zigged to port, toward the submarine, and reduced the range to a thousand yards. Commander McClintock was glued to the periscope. The shooting bearing—the relative position between sub and target that must exist when the torpedoes were launched—was coming up.

"Stand-by—Mark!" cried Mr. Wilkinson from the TDC.

"Fire one!" ordered the skipper. "Fire one!" repeated Clay into the phone, and he heard the talker in the forward torpedo room repeat the words. The torpedo officer had pressed a firing key in the conning tower when the skipper had given the word, but since firing circuits could fail, the firing order also was transmitted by the infallible sound-powered phones, so that the men in the torpedo room could fire the fish by hand if necessary. Clay could feel the boat jerk as the first torpedo surged from the tube, lightening the vessel by three thousand pounds. Five more torpedoes quickly followed the first.

"Running hot, straight and normal, sir," reported the man at the sound gear.

"Come hard left!" ordered McClintock, as soon as the last

torpedo had left the tubes. "Shift targets to second vessel in the column, Gene." Even as the sub turned away, reversing itself to bring the stern tubes to bear, the skipper ran the periscope up for a quick bearing sight. He called it off and brought the periscope down again.

"Give me a range!" cried Gene Wilkinson from the torpedo data computer. "You can't shoot without a range!"

"Range, fifteen hundred," McClintock told him.

In the hot, crowded little space of the conning tower, officers and men stood tense and alert.

"Hurry it up!" growled McClintock from the periscope. A moment more crawled by.

"TDC ready!" sang out Wilkinson. The boat had nearly completed her turn, and the firing bearing was approaching.

"Fire seven!" McClintock shouted, and the first stern tube emptied a fish toward the enemy. Just then heavy underwater explosions were heard—a series of them that continued as the remaining three torpedoes left the tubes.

"Depth charges, Dave?" asked the Exec.

McClintock shook his head. "Those were our torpedoes hitting," he said quietly.

McClintock swung the periscope back toward the first target, and Clay saw him stiffen. There was awe in his face as he stepped back from the scope. He caught Clay's eye and motioned toward the periscope.

"Take a look, Harkness. It's a sight to remember."

Clay moved eagerly up to the periscope and looked in. The sight struck him like a physical blow. The cruiser was spouting flame from her forward turret to her stern; she was shattered and sinking, with dense black smoke from burning oil rising over her. Her bow already was under. Clay swung the periscope to the next vessel; she too was afire and listing heavily, dead in the water. Dazed, Clay stepped away from the scope, releasing it to the skipper.

"Take her down," McClintock said calmly. "Rig for silent running. There'll be destroyers overhead in a minute."

As the sub went further down, the crew heard more distant explosions, not depth charges. They knew that the *Dace* also was hitting the target. *Dace* had, in fact, sunk another heavy cruiser. The breaking-up noises from the *Darter's* sinking victim came through the sub's hull with ghastly clarity. The men could hear the crushing of plates, the rumble of waters, the crackling and groaning of metal going down, down, down. Then the destroyers arrived.

"Four of them making a run now, Captain!" the sound man reported, his face pale in the strong light. The crew didn't need to be told. Clay could hear the destroyers' propellers, like an electric razor at work on a two-day beard. Then came the *click-wham! click-wham!* of the depth charges, none dangerously close. The boat shook, lights dimmed and came on again, bits of cork fell from the insulation and dust floated in the wet, hot air.

The depth charges went on for an hour and a half. After an additional precautionary wait, the *Darter* came to periscope depth. The Japanese fleet was gone, except for one crippled cruiser—*Darter's* second target—guarded by two destroyers and two aircraft. A daylight attack on her would be impossible; but during the day they would track her submerged, and in the night finish her off.

Clay finally fell asleep, still disturbed by memory of the sinking ship. *Darter* had scored before this, but not on so large a scale, and Clay had seen only one merchantman go down.

At midnight, *Darter* and *Dace* were sneaking down Palawan Straits at seventeen knots, well separated so they could make attacks from different directions on the doomed cruiser. Clay Harkness was again on the bridge as lookout, his surface battle station. The captain was standing beside him; the navigator was in the conning tower, keeping bearings and fixes. The night was dark and hot. Clay felt the sweat running down his face as he peered ceaselessly through the binoculars, sweeping his sector without pause.

"Position before long," McClintock remarked calmly. "We must be getting close to her now."

Then ultimate disaster struck. Clay felt a jar, not a heavy one, and then had the distinct and awful feeling that the submarine was riding up on something. He felt the bow tilt upward, and then there was a shuddering crash. Clay was flung against the forward bulwark; the officer of the deck fell flat, and from below came thuds, crashes and shouts. Then everyone was quiet in the submariner's instinctive reaction to danger.

"What was that?" the navigator yelled frantically, as he came scrambling up onto the bridge.

"We're aground," McClintock said grimly. Clay Harkness

was too stunned even to feel. Aground! In an enemy sea, with enemies all around. Aground!

"Captain, we can't be aground!" the navigator cried. "The nearest land is nineteen miles away!"

"An uncharted reef," said McClintock.

"Bridge!" It was the voice of the radar officer. "Japanese vessel, probably a destroyer, coming our way. Range, fifteen thousand yards."

At that dreadful word, Clay and the others on the bridge froze in momentary despair. Then noise of any kind ceased; the hatch was closed, and even the binnacle light was covered with a jacket. Clay felt totally exposed. If the Jap destroyer found them, they were gone, dead, finished.

"Range, fourteen thousand," came the murmured word from below. Seven miles, Clay thought sickly. A long way for some things, a long way to swin, to walk. But not a long way for death to travel at twenty knots. The submarine felt like a concrete building under Clay's feet. There was not the slightest motion; that fact and the submarine's unnatural, upward tilt indicated that the boat was far up on the slanting reef.

"Thirteen thousand, Captain."

"Get the gun crew topside, quietly," McClintock ordered. The four-inch deck gun would be useless, Clay knew, but the captain would go down fighting.

"Twelve thousand, Captain." Step by step, yard by yard, destiny was approaching the *Darter*. Then a new note came to the radar officer's voice.

"He's turned away, Captain. Range thirteen thousand!"

A murmured cheer went up, fervent in spite of its quietness. In ten minutes the destroyer was at fifteen thousand yards and going away rapidly.

"Okay," said the captain in relief. Then he turned his attention to the problem at hand. "Earnest, start throwing everything movable overboard." He leaned over the hatch and shouted down for the radio operator to try to raise the *Dace*.

The next few moments were endless. What if the *Dace* didn't answer? What if she were in trouble, maybe aground too, maybe out of range, driven down—anything? The suspense was a tangible thing, for the other submarine represented the only possible hope for the crew of the *Darter*.

Then the answer came. "I've got her loud and clear, Skipper. She's on her way!"

Everybody aboard smiled when they heard the news; Clay felt as if he were going to cry. Then all hands went back to lightening the ship. The torpedoes were fired away from the stern tubes; benches, chairs, tables, personal gear, food were dumped over the side. They tried to rock her as the tide came in, men running back and forth, together, engines going flank speed astern. The *Dace* came sliding in out of the darkness. She passed a towline and tried to haul her sister sub free.

"No use, boys," said McClintock, sadly. "It's time for us to leave her."

They transferred aboard the *Dace*. All equipment aboard the *Darter* was smashed, and demolition charges set. McClintock came last of all. He stood by Clay, briefly, on the *Dace*'s crowded bridge, staring back at his ship waiting for destruction.

"Good-bye, *Darter*," he said, quietly. "You were a good old girl."

Then the *Dace* turned away into the night, and before dawn she submerged with two full crews aboard.

Darter was lost. But she cost the enemy a heavy cruiser sunk and another put out of the battle. Most important, the contact report told the American commanders where the main body of enemy strength lay. They knew the direction from which the main blow would come.

Darter had reduced the force of that blow by a little, and the thought cheered Clay Harkness as he lay in a strange bunk on the *Dace* and heard the waters rushing by the steel hull as the submarine headed for home, leaving the coming battle behind.

Through the blue seas the Japanese forces gathered. Around Leyte Gulf American planes and ships kept watch for the red and white battle flag of Japan.

THREE

AIR ATTACK

THE DAWN OF OCTOBER 24 was beginning to lighten the sky in the east as the Japanese forces moved closer to the great tangle of islands, reefs and seas soon to become a battleground. The largest Japanese fleet, the Central Force, continued to steam northward. Its commander, Admiral Kurita, was angered and saddened by the losses the *Dace* and *Darter* had inflicted, but he was determined to follow his orders to the end in this final, mighty effort of the Japanese Navy. Kurita commanded five battleships, eleven heavy cruisers, two light cruisers and nineteen destroyers. He was to pass through San Bernardino Strait that night and enter Leyte Gulf at dawn on the twenty-fifth shooting.

A small part of Kurita's force, under command of Admiral Nishimuru, had already broken off. At Mindoro it would join another force under Admiral Shima, which had proceeded there from the inland Sea of Japan. This combined force—two battleships, three heavy cruisers, one light cruiser and eight destroyers—would pass through Surigao Strait on the night of the twenty-fourth and emerge into Leyte Gulf at dawn.

A third Japanese force, commanded by Admiral Ozawa, was also steaming to the scene from the Inland Sea. This force consisted of four carriers, two converted battleships, three light cruisers and eight destroyers. Ozawa expected that his Northern Force would be destroyed; so did the Japanese High Command. They had put the ships out as a sacrifice to draw the ships and planes of Admiral Halsey's Third Fleet away from Leyte Gulf.

The combined Japanese fleet was a potent naval armada. It had virtually no air cover, but if Halsey could be drawn off by the sitting ducks of Ozawa, the American invasion fleet might well be destroyed. During the night, the Japanese commanders continued on their assigned missions, drawing toward Leyte Gulf, where American ships lay in serried rows awaiting the dawn.

Larry White had slept soundly, but he was always ready for the clanging gong to come, the General Quarters that would lift him from sleep. At dawn the ship would be awake and ready for trouble. When the dark silence, red-tinged from the dim battle lights, was split by harsh white light, the clanging alarm and the loud voice of the boatswain's mate over the PA system: "Now hear this! General Quarters! Man your battle stations," he was over the side of his bunk and getting into dungarees before he knew himself awake. The men about him were dull with sleep. They didn't rush too much with their dressing, for this was an air crew compartment and no guns awaited them.

When he emerged on the vast space of the flight deck, Larry paused a moment to breathe the fresh, warm air. Some clouds were in the sky, but he could see stars between them. The *Lexington* rolled like a great, flat-topped whale, and he heard the wash of waves above the soft drone of the stacks. Then he stepped inside the clean, familiar space of the air crew ready room. His things were on a hook—Mae West life jacket, .38 revolver, cartridge belt, knife, helmet, flight suit. He put on the suit and the Mae West and then found the comfortable chair with his name on the back. This was only the dawn alert; no planes would be manned except for the first combat air patrol of the day. This patrol would be taking off soon, followed by the morning aircraft search. Like most of the men around him, Larry leaned back in the chair and began to relapse into sleep.

"Why do they get us up here this time of day, anyway?" Bill Mackey grumbled. "I like my sack below a heck of a lot better."

Gunner's Mate, first class, Ronald, an old hand, looked at

Bill sardonically. "Look, Boot, we have dawn GQ because that's a sub's favorite time for popping you with a fish—get you against the light. Planes that've been shadowing all night can see well enough for a bombing run. Suppose the old Blue Goose gets a torpedo in her belly—you want to be able to take the planes off, or not? Might not be much time."

"I know, I know. Okay, they're right—but can't a man gripe a little?"

"I reckon you can, Bill." Larry said, grinning. "Now shut up. I want to take a nap."

At 0630 hours the *Lexington* secured from General Quarters, but before the air crews were released for breakfast, Lieutenant Commander McGowan, skipper of the dive-bombing group aboard, came pushing briskly into the room. He waved the rising men back into their seats, muttered something to the crew chief and then started talking.

"Work today, boys. Eat a good breakfast. We'll be taking off shortly afterward. There's a big force, very big, coming from the southwest, and another smaller one from the northwest. We've had snoopers around during the night. Combat air patrol will be doubled. Don't know which force will be our meat, but I expect it will be the one to the southwest. Eat hearty. It will be a long day. And, boys . . ." He hesitated, was silent. "This is the big one. Make it good."

"Maybe I'm not so hungry after all," Bill Mackey said. "Kinda scared. The skipper looked solemn."

"Let's go try, anyway," Larry answered. "I could use some orange juice and ham and eggs."

Larry ate well in the noisy, cheerful crew's mess room. He'd learned not to think about what might be ahead when he was having breakfast on a day like this. Thinking about it would make his stomach queasy, and he knew he would need the food before the day was out. He'd strap himself in the rear cockpit of the SB2C dive bomber and face forward while Lieutenant Howard took her off the deck. If nothing went wrong, he'd swing the seat around, hoist out the pair of thirty-caliber machine guns, get radio contact with the ship and with the air group leader and squadron leader and then ride backward into battle, looking at where he'd been instead of where he was going. When they found a target, he would ride backward down the steep incline of air, shooting at Zeroes if they followed the Helldiver down, holding his breath with the scream and rush of the dive, half blacking out when the plant dropped the big bomb to swoop up again, facing the enemy planes and heading for cloud cover. Then back to the carrier, if it could be found; and then land on it, if it was still intact and if the plane itself held together. Larry found his throat tightening, hindering the ham and eggs. He realized he'd been thinking ahead and shoved his mind back to grouse season down on the edge of the Salisbury Swamp.

During dawn GQ, the *Lexington* had launched a dozen dive bombers and fighters for searches beyond Luzon. Larry's squadron had had search duty the day before; they were in the strike team today. After breakfast, the air crews went back to their ready rooms, taut and prepared.

At 0822 the word came through that a very strong force of

enemy ships had been found south of Mindoro, heading for San Bernardino Strait. Admiral Halsey, Commander, Third Fleet, at once ordered his three fast carrier groups to concentrate off San Bernardino Strait, streaming at flank speed to the westward to reduce distance for their strike planes. Larry White settled back into his chair in the ready room and tried to concentrate on a magazine. His gear was ready; he had the frequencies all set on his board, and the guns in the plane had been cleaned and checked the night before. Nothing left to do but wait—and sweat, even though the ready room was air conditioned.

The PA system blared: "Many Bogeys approaching ship. Fighter pilots, man your planes. Fighter pilots, man your planes!"

Men in the ready room looked at each other, listening to the savage roar of engines from outside, the distant shouts, the crescendo of a fighter being revved just outside the door. They stayed in their places; at this moment the flight deck would be a crowded, hectic place, with no room for sightseers. Fighter after fighter roared by while the *Lex* shook with the increased speed demanded by flight operations and the fight to come. When the last fighter of this section was launched, Larry and several others went outside, hovering close to the door, through which they could dive for shelter.

All about, the sea was dotted with the orderly array of ships: two big carriers, the *Lexington* and the *Essex,* and the light carrier *Princeton.* Behind each carrier two plane-guard destroyers hovered, ready to pick up any airman who fell in the drink taking off or landing. In a circular disposition around the carriers were the destroyers of the screen; far astern were battleships and cruisers, ready to meet any challenging surface forces. These vessels did not cluster close to the carriers to aid them with AA fire against the coming attack. The carriers had their own shields—the vees and diamonds of Hellcat fighters circling high above; some of the fighters were already out of sight, being vectored out by Combat Information Center to meet the oncoming enemy attack.

"Ahead, to port," Bill Mackey said, grabbing Larry's arm. "They've caught 'em!"

Larry looked, then stiffened. He saw no less than three downward plunging trails of smoke, marking where burning planes hurtled toward the sea. Others followed; even at this distance he could hear the straining pull of motors, the eerie scream of divided air and the staccato, brief-spaced sound of machine-gun fire. The fight swirled closer. Shooting broke out off the starboard bow. In the gun galleries and turrets of the *Lexington* eager men sat with eyes on telescope sights or radar fire control dials, fingers ready for firing buttons. The forty-millimeter quadruple mounts, the twenty-millimeter, the five-inch thirty-eights—all ready, all without targets. But in the distance the rattle, streak and roar of the battles where men were dying in plunging planes moved closed.

But it never arrived. Fight after fight started, blazed, moved closer and faded away. The Hellcats were mincing the Japanese attacks before they could strike home. Larry could hardly speak for excitement and pride. Those fighter boys, those

39

young, careless, crazy officers, those fighters! They were really doing a job!

At 0938 the battle stopped being a spectator sport. The carrier group had just turned into the wind to recover planes, and Larry and Bill were exchanging happy grins when Larry suddenly saw a glint of silver close above the stern of the *Princeton,* a thousand yards away.

"Look out!" he cried. "There's a. . . ."

The explosion shook him, and a great shock of flame burst up from the *Princeton;* fragments blew outward, then vast gouts of black smoke expanded into the air like black, irregular balloons. Mouth open, Larry saw one of the big plane elevators soar into the air as high as the carrier's masthead, then drop back into smoke and flame. His stomach heaved at the sight. In moments the *Princeton* was nearly dead in the water, still heading into the wind, and the smoke, like a black mantle, spread astern and above.

In a few minutes the remainder of the fast carrier group cleared the area, leaving three destroyers and a cruiser to render assistance to the lost ship and her crew. When the black smoke was only a smudge on the horizon, the *Lexington* swung her bow into the wind. "Launch Strike!" the PA roared. "Pilots! Man your planes!"

The clock had ticked, the hands swung; for Larry and the rest of his dive-bomber squadron, the time for action was now.

The flight deck looked far below Larry; the SB2C had a high lift to her. With the canopy slid forward, he was exposed to air and wind down to the waist. He'd made his checks. The guns were ready, with the belts coiled down in the ready cans; the radio was warmed up, and air control had checked his settings and answered five by five. He had fastened his seat belt, but not buckled on the parachute. Within minutes the Helldiver would be lunging upward from the flight deck at the bow of the carrier. The slightest stuttering or faltering of the engine would lay her in the drink, and then there would be seconds to live, to get out of the plane before she went down and wait for the plane guard destroyers to slice up alongside.

Two more SB2C's were ahead on the flight deck; the skipper's was at the line now. The control officer was at that moment waving his flag in a tight circle, increasing in speed—the signal to rev up the engine. The engine's noise grew to a thunderous road; wind and prop wash tore across the flight deck, molding the flight deck crews' dungaree trousers close against their legs. Their varicolored cloth helmets, colored according to job, clung tight to heads. Others on deck held to caps with both hands, staggering in the blast. The control officer's flag stopped; then he swung it forward in a sweeping motion. The dive bomber, vibrating against its brakes, started rolling forward. Instantly the plane behind it edged forward. Larry felt his own machine move, its whirling prop only a foot or two behind the tail of the preceding plane. Again the thunder, the shaking, straining; then that plane was gone, slow roll changing to fast dash, wheels lifting from the deck only yards from the forward end. It climbed and banked away to the right.

Now Larry's dive bomber was at the mark. He hunched over, one hand on the release of the seat belt, the other on the life-jacket valve. He was lost in that intense inner communion of the man about to take off from a carrier's flight deck, when death could occur within the next twenty seconds. The control officer's flag was whirling. Larry felt the brute machine beneath him straining and trembling at the brakes; the full seventeen hundred horsepower leashed and balked. He looked ahead past his pilot's helmet, the windscreen, the bow of the carrier. There was a big ground swell, and the bow of the flat-top rose and fell a good thirty feet with the waves. Leave it at the wrong instant with bow pointed down, and a plane might easily plow into the next wave, smash, crash, and be gone into the thousand-fathom depth, its crew still crouched within it.

The flag stopped whirling, and swung to point ahead. The plane moved, at first agonizingly slow, then faster, faster. Click, click, click, bump, the cleats of the deck hurtling beneath the wheels, ever faster. The superstructure a blue blur, the sun bright, sky blue, life flashing past, blurred figures of men, then. . . .

Not dropping at all, the plane cleared the end of the deck. Larry felt the wheels clear, felt the smooth cushion of air a second before the deck ended. Then the plane was swinging to the right and climbing. He heard the whine of the gear as the wheels came up, the thump of their housing as the dive bomber swung alongside the carrier a hundred yards to the right. The carrier dropped rapidly below it, and another plane was even now hurtling toward the flight deck's end.

Larry let out his breath. A hundred times before, two hundred, he had sat like this, fingers twitching, his life helplessly in the skill and hands of another man. He would never get used to it. *That* fear, *that* danger, was gone for the moment. Now for the others.

Larry flipped the lock and swung his seat around, facing aft. He buckled on his parachute pack. He heaved up the guns on their ring mount, flipped up the sights and worked the two charging handles. He clicked on the safety. A little later he'd ask his pilot for permission to test guns. Now he would sit quietly and wait. In the headphones the terse chatter of the strike pulsed and crackled. "Over." "Roger and Out." "Here, Pete, on your tail. Roger, Skipper." "Right behind you, Buster. Red flight, red flight." "Peckerwoods from tree, fall in, fall in."

These pilots were old hands now. Very quickly the chatter died away and the strike lined out to the west. Larry looked around at the planes. Combat air patrol, search flights, and troop support ashore had thinned the ranks. Ahead and above were eight Hellcats, Grumman fighters. The Curtiss SB2C Larry rode was leading a section of five dive bombers. Below and aft, the sleek shapes of eleven Grumman TBF's, torpedo planes, were in close formation. A cloud drew a cold gray mist around them all; then they emerged into the sun again, the motors still at the pitch of climb. Below the glinting sea looked like blue, corrugated tin; cloud puffs filled the sky, and to the right, a green island was approaching and dropping.

The mountains of Luzon were passing beneath the plane,

now at about six thousand feet. He looked at his watch in shock. Nearly an hour gone.

"About forty minutes to go, Larry." Lieutenant Howard's calm voice sounded in the intercom. "Test your guns. And keep loose, Vermonter." They had been together for nearly eight months. Larry knew Mister Howard trusted him and relied on him; and he in turn placed his life in the long, thin fingers of the gangling Ohio man without any hesitation, time after time, day after day. Larry had heard things that jerks back home had said about the caste system, and officers and enlisted men. The man up forward there had all the responsibility; his hands did the delicate and amazing work of control; his mind, unflurried by danger, death or excitement, had to work out the delicate problems of wind, course, drift and compass error to bring the two of them, and their plane, back to the doubtful safety of the flight deck that moved from place to place, was attacked and threatened and changed course, speed and intention. Mister Howard had to bring plane and ship together and bring the plane down. And he was as friendly to Larry as anyone had ever been. Larry knew he could go to him anytime, for any reason, and find sympathy and prompt, forceful help.

Thinking this, Larry swung the guns to the side, pointing clear of the formation. He flipped off the safety and pressed the trigger bar. The guns purred, the mount absorbing most of the recoil, the muzzles climbing a little and to the right.

"Guns checked, skipper," Larry said, seeing that the switch was on intercom.

"Okay. Reports are that we'll find no air opposition. Just Ack Ack. Cream off the bridge when we pull out of the dive. We'll pick a nice fat one."

"Roger Wilco, *Sir.*"

"Don't sir me, you Vermont apple knocker. What's that at twelve o'clock high? A Hellcat?"

"Yes sir. Nice to see him there."

Now they were over the Sibuyan Sea. The sea was a deep blue, flecked with silver and dotted with islands. Each island was surrounded with a spectrum of light gray, green, greener bluish, blue and then purple where the bottom fell away. Larry wondered if Mister Howard would let him fly the plane home. He did so often, if there were no complications. Larry had his application for flight training in already, and his chances looked good.

Suddenly he was sick; he had let his mind slip ahead to the dive through a garden of black and red AA bursts. He forced it up to Silver Lake, in May. He had a casting rod in his hand and his boots and lunch on his back. A white-throated sparrow was singing in a hemlock thicket, and the night crawlers in the bait can were strong and greasy. The trout would be waiting. He'd go over to the east bank, among the driftwood and downed trees, to a big rock. He'd try the Meps spinner first; if they didn't take that, he'd put on a gob of worm and a sinker, throw the bait well out, put the rod in a forked stick and lie on his back with the spring sun on him and wait for the line to twitch.

Thunder ahead, above the roar and throb of the engine.

Larry shoved the canopy away. Wind howled and tore at him, but the thunder throbbed louder. In the air ahead he saw black blossoms and silver glints. In the ocean beneath, black smoke and white smoke curled and rose. Things moved on the water, drawing white carpets after them and winking red at the sky. Silver bugs streaked downward, soared upward. He saw torpedo planes beneath, very low, moving in.

He looked at his watch. It was 1330. One-thirty in the afternoon on this day that his life might end, this October 24.

"Peckerwood Flight from Deadwood," said the radio in his ear. He tensed. "See the big fat battleship bearing 190, relative. No air opposition. Split up. Section One, take her from the bow, Section Two from the rear. And don't bump heads when you pull out."

He heard the other pilots and Mister Howard answer, then felt his plane swerve right, followed by two other dive bombers. He gulped. Now he must forget the ship for a while. He stopped craning around and instead looked astern, looked high. Maybe no air opposition, but Zeroes could appear mighty suddenly, and they'd dive on the bomber from the rear and high if they did appear. His job now was to make them slide down a current of machine-gun bullets if they tried—six hundred rounds a minute from each of the two Browning thirties.

"Stand by, Larry-Oh," came Howard's tight voice. "Suck in your gut, boy. Here we go!"

Oh God, if ever I . . . if ever I. . . . Be with us. . . .

The tail whipped up slowly, it seemed. Facing backward,

Larry plunged down. He pressed his head against the rest, held the guns tightly, kept his eyes astern. No weight, the world falling beneath him, his body lifted from the surface of the chute pack as the plane accelerated from beneath him, falling, falling, faster, faster, black specks, a sudden burst of black and red astern of them, to one side of them; two other planes behind them, the good familiar forms of the SB2C's of the section. Faster, and faster, the end of the world maybe seconds away. Not knowing it, he shouted something as he saw black and red and silver plane coincide, and the first plane after him wheeled away, sideways, red growing from it, black streaming from it, silver of separated wing, and he was sick, sick and falling falling, falling. . . .

Then he weighed a ton; a black screen, red-tinged, drew over his eyes, the seat was half a vise's jaws, the other half something unseen but as hard, harder, the force. . . . He drifted, the screen lifted. His stomach kept going downward, but the plane was climbing. Looking straight back, he saw the awesome length and bulk of the battleship, twinkling with red fires. Black puffs appeared all around him, the climbing plane leaped and buffeted in the pressures, the explosions. He felt her lurch harder, felt something hit her, heard somehow glass shattering, smelled strange smells and saw strange visions; saw then the monstrous red and white blast on the battleship's deck astern, the vast burst of black smoke. The bomb had hit!

"We hit her, Mister Howard, we hit her. Right on the fantail!"

"Wow! And wow again! But we're hit too, Larry. They

47

busted my compass and my canopy. And the oil pressure doesn't look so good. We hit her, huh?"

They were level now and high again, the vast drop and climb finished. Black puffs around them. Larry saw, in the distance, the red-black trail of a burning, plummeting plane.

Then the battle was behind them, they were away, alone, in silence that the engine's roar only accentuated.

"We're . . . we're hit, sir?" Larry said through stiff lips.

"Yes. I've got the canopy in my lap, and the compass is gone. We'll head east. We've got so many carriers over there we can't miss—if the oil pressure holds."

"Oil pressure?"

"Yep. Guess the Japs got an oil line. Dropping—very slowly though. She'll fly, she'll fly. Don't know how long, but she'll fly. We won't wait to rendezvous—just haul tail. Hang on to that rabbit's foot, junior."

For the next hour and a half, Larry needed all the magic of the hills to keep him calm. For the first hour all seemed quite normal; the islands showed the way, and the sun itself. Then he began to notice the smell of leaking oil and heating metal.

"How's the oil pressure, Mister Howard?" he croaked.

"Going down, Larry. We've still got some time left, and Luzon is under us now. We ought to sight a carrier soon, any carrier. When we do, we squat."

Another twenty minutes. Larry was thinking about snow shoeing up by Silver Lake, hunting the big winter rabbits.

And ice fishing. The funny way the water doesn't come rushing up out onto the ice when you chop a hole through two feet of it, the way you'd think it would. Just stops, level with the top. And.... He saw something. He yelled:

"Carrier, dead ahead! Carrier!"

"Where? Ah.... You're right, for sure, Larry. And there's another—another. A carrier group. Not ours—they're escort carriers, baby flat-tops. But they're big enough for us. If we can get her down now, we'll even save the engine. Red line's just getting up to the danger mark. Fasten the seat belt; we're going down."

The radio was dead, along with the compass, but Mister Howard flew the plane one full circle around the ship, flaps down. Alongside her bridge, Larry fired a red Very star. Then they could see the landing signal officer aft waving another plane away, and they knew the deck was open for them. The dive bomber swung around the stern, dropping fast. She banked and came in line with the carrier. Accustomed to the *Lexington*'s great flight deck, Larry didn't think Mister Howard could ever put her down on this heaving postage stamp. Now the plane was in the groove, dropping, sliding down the invisible wire she must ride. The signal officer's bright paddles were level, held at arm's length. The right paddle dipped; Larry felt the pilot bank the plane a little left in correction. The paddles sank, lower, lower. The plane dropped. The stern of the flight deck heaved up on a wave, dropped again. It was a hundred yards ahead, and now the fuselage of the plane blocked the deck out completely, leaving only the landing signal officer standing on his platform on the outboard, after corner.

The paddle whipped inward across the man's throat; Howard cut the throttles. Larry held on tight, seeing the deck shoot up to meet them, feeling his stomach empty in empty air as the plane dropped from beneath them. Then the dive bomber was on the deck, bumping, bouncing. Then, jerked down by the restraining wire, it hauled to a quick, jerky stop. The tail wheel hit the deck with a thud, and Larry breathed again. The hook man dived beneath the plane, loosing tail hook from cable. Then Howard taxied the plane forward, following a rapidly backing and beckoning man in a green helmet. She rolled to a stop on a plane elevator; at the signal, Howard cut the ignition.

"Well, Larry," he said. "It ain't home, but I'm glad to be here. We laid an egg on that battleship, didn't you say? Wow!"

Men helped them out of the cockpit; a young officer came up to them. He introduced himself. Howard's word of explanation satisfied him at once—it was a common thing for a damaged or lost plane to come down on the wrong carrier. He took them up to the captain, who greeted Howard warmly and was anxious to hear about the strike. It turned out that he knew more about it than they, since he'd been reading strike reports all afternoon. The American planes had sunk a super battleship, the *Musashi*. The *Yamamoto* had been hit at least twice—"That's us, Larry," Mister Howard said, poking his gunner-radioman in the ribs. "That's the one we laid the egg on!"

"Good work," said the captain. "A lot of other hits reported —cruisers and destroyers. When the last plane left, the whole Japanese force had turned tail and was heading west. Little too much for them, I expect."

"Man! I mean, sir, we must have really smeared 'em."

"Hmm. No doubt about *Musashi,* I guess. But I doubt the force is hurt otherwise as much as the reports say. You know what aviators are like, boys—and so do I. I'm one myself, you know. Now, how about your plane? Damaged badly?"

"They've got her down in repair now, sir. I asked Mr. Hillis to get off an arrival message for us to the *Lex;* if she's not too far off and we can get filled up with oil, I'd like to get back. Might be another strike tomorrow."

"You're right. There may well be. Mr. Jenkins? Find out about Mister Howard's plane, please. Now, Mister Howard, how about a cup of coffee and a bite to eat? Send your gunner down to the crew's mess; they'll fix him up with something."

The dive bomber was only slightly injured; one oil line had been cut by fragments, and the power cable feeding compass and radio had been shorted out. By the time Larry and Mister Howard had eaten, the dive bomber was ready to go. Following the messenger sent down to get him, Larry was surprised to hear his name called. He whirled around just in time to be grabbed in heavy hands.

"Larry! Larry White! Call me a Boston Mick if it ain't!"

"Well, for the love of Mike! Old Tom Bellido! I didn't know you were on the *Gambier Bay!*"

"Best carrier in the fleet. You'd think an airdale would know that! Sticking around awhile?"

"Just taking off. Got to get back to a real carrier—the *Lexington*—and get on with the war. Good seeing you, Tom."

"Same for you, Larry. Look, let's get together when the fleet gets back to Ulithi—if that's where we end up. See how many of the old gang we can dig up."

"Are any of them around?"

They were on the flight deck now, talking as they walked. Tom stopped and swung Larry around.

"See that destroyer out there? That's the *Johnston*. Einar Andersen is chief quartermaster in her."

"Wonderful! Wouldn't it be swell to see the old square head again?"

"I see him every now and then—the *Johnston* has been acting as plane guard for us."

"I hear Clay Harkness is on a sub, somewhere around. And I think Jerry is riding one of the PT boats. Anyway, he was the last I heard from him."

"Good. We'll make that a date at Ulithi. Nice to have had you aboard."

Tom stood under the wing of the scarred dive bomber while Larry climbed into his place. Larry waved down at Tom, then settled himself into the seat, fighting down the old fear, made stronger by the narrow escape he and Mister Howard had had.

52

Seventeen holes in the plane, but they'd made it back to the *Gambier Bay,* and would make it back to the *Lexington.* Mister Howard had the course to rendezvous, and the *Lex* was only thirty minutes' flight away.

The dive bomber ran out of deck before she was fully airborne and dropped six feet after she cleared the bow, bringing Larry's heart into his throat again. Then she was climbing, circling to the right, banking, the wheels coming up. Mister Howard circled once above the carrier. Larry thought he could make out Tom standing down there on the flight deck. Then the dive bomber lined away to the southwest. Well before sunset, they'd be home on the *Lexington* again.

Larry settled back in his seat, took up his watch of the rear half of the horizon and thought about home.

When that sun did set, Larry White was eating dinner at the table in his own mess, excused from evening General Quarters along with the rest of the strike air crew. Three planes had failed to return, and Larry felt sad and empty, seeing the vacant places of men he had known.

His grief was mixed with exultation as he learned the results of the day's battle. The Americans were far ahead on the balance of losses. The *Princeton* had gone down, and the *Birmingham,* a heavy cruiser, had been badly damaged while alongside helping to fight fires. But the Japanese had lost two heavy cruisers to the submarines, with a third badly damaged and sent home. In the air strikes of October 24, the Japanese had lost the great battleship *Musashi,* and a heavy

53

cruiser so badly damaged that she had been sent back to Borneo. They had also lost over a hundred planes in air attacks on the carriers that morning, while American plane losses had been limited to eighteen craft. Victory's balance was swinging to the American Navy—but it could swing back. The Japanese forces were still powerful and resolute.

When darkness came, soldiers ashore paused for the night in hastily dug foxholes; the last plane landed on the last carrier. A semi-quiet settled over the great area. Stars glimmered between the darkness of rain squalls marching over the sea.

But the springs of action coiled tighter and tighter, and the intermission would not last. Search planes had now spotted Admiral Ozawa's Northern Force, with its four carriers, cruisers and destroyers. When Admiral Halsey was informed that the Jap force to the north had four carriers in it, he knew what he had to do. Carrier planes had been among those attacking his air groups during the day; they must have come from the Northern Force. "Get the carriers" had always been his battle cry. And there was no danger from the Center Force, for his beloved Third Fleet airdales had mauled it and sent it packing toward Japan for repairs and reinforcements.

Admiral Halsey made his decision. At 8:22 P.M. on October 24, he ordered all units of the Third Fleet to move north at twenty-five knots, to find Ozawa and the carriers and destroy them. Hoping for surface action, Halsey took along the fast battleships as well. By midnight, battleships and carriers were tearing northward, just as the Japanese had planned. And at that hour, Kurita and his Center Force were emerging from San Bernardino Strait, unopposed, unseen.

Also at midnight, Admirals Nishimuru and Shima and their fleets were very busy. They were not having an easy passage of the Surigao Strait.

FOUR

SUNSET FOR CARRIERS

BATTLESHIPS, CRUISERS, DESTROYERS and carriers raced through the somber night toward the enemy. At midnight, Admiral Halsey returned the tactical command of Task Force Thirty-Eight to Admiral Marc Mitscher, with orders to sink the enemy carriers and as many other ships as possible. During the hours while Halsey handled the entire fleet, Mitscher had been only a passenger aboard the *Lexington*. Now this small, wrinkled admiral, the aviators' favorite flag officer, began with the expert's sure hand to prepare the destruction of the enemy fleet.

While the fleet steamed northward, Larry White slept soundly, mind and body exhausted by the activity and strain of the day before. The rest revived his youthful body, and after the first shock of the 5 A.M. awakening had worn off, he felt fine. He ate breakfast hungrily, with only an occasional thought of what lay ahead. After breakfast he walked through the pre-dawn flight deck darkness to the ready room. The flight deck was alive with activity as planes were brought up from below and spotted for takeoff—fighters forward, then dive bombers, then torpedo planes. The planes were being armed with heavy bombs and torpedoes; Larry gulped a little as a dolly load of 500-pound bombs wheeled by him. He knew that bombs like that would be nestled under the wings of his aircraft when it rolled forward on the flight deck and took to the air again.

Excitement moved through the ready room. The word was out to the flyers that this time they were after carriers, the biggest of all game to a naval aviator. It had been months since these men had hit carriers, and they were ready. They knew that if they wiped out these enemy ships, Japan would be out of carriers and their own futures would be safer during the rest of the war.

Larry had barely settled into his chair when the harsh word came: "Pilots, man your planes!"

It was all so familiar—the hand at his elbow as he mounted the wing, the crewman slapping his back as he settled into the cockpit, Mister Howard's quiet, "Well, Larry, here we go again." Just barely dawn.

"They found 'em, Mister Howard?" Larry asked over intercom.

"They think so, but they haven't fixed their exact location. We're going to orbit about fifty miles north and wait for a positive contact. The Old Man knows the direction, you see, but not the distance."

Larry had done this hundreds of times before, but still he felt the suspense, the tenseness. Then the plane was in the air and forming up with the rest of the strike force.

At 0653 Larry's plane was circling with the entire strike force over empty ocean. Larry was tense but calm, knowing the waiting might go on for some time. His thoughts went back to the four friends of boot camp days. He knew that several of them were somewhere in the area. He thought of Einar, and of Tom Bellido, in the same escort carrier group.

As Larry remembered these two, the lookouts on Admiral Sprague's flagship were sighting the masts of Kurita's battleships. But no ripples from that action crossed the hundreds of miles to where Larry White circled empty sea in a dive bomber's rear cockpit.

Larry heard the first contact report go in to the *Lexington*: the enemy fleet has been found, about eighty miles to the north. The air group commander's plane led the way out of the circle. Mister Howard was humming rather tunelessly over the intercom. Larry looked at his watch. It was ten minutes after seven, and the sun was blazing golden over the vast area of blue sea. He gulped down his heart, got guns tested and ready and sat back to wait.

He felt almost sorry for the Japanese as the strike force moved swiftly toward battle. The American search planes were circling above the enemy fleet, describing ships, numbers, types.

"No air," one pilot reported. "Only a few acrobats, but they don't want to bother us, apparently. Sitting ducks, boys! Come get them!"

Larry was puzzled by this report. Four carriers? Two battleships converted to semi-carriers? And no planes? He began to feel uneasy again. This must be a trap; surely the enemy planes were somewhere about, possibly vectored out to meet this strike he was a part of. He redoubled his search of the sky, especially around the rising sun.

It was a trap, of course, or part of one. But the trap wasn't set for the planes of Task Force Thirty-Eight. Instead it was set for the shipping in Leyte Gulf and for the American escort carriers. Larry was approaching the bait; the jaws of the trap were at that moment closing, apparently with all success, around the destroyers and carriers of Taffy Three. Ozawa's force was sent to considered, certain destruction, with very few planes. Almost all he had, had been expended the previous day in the attacks on the *Lexington*'s carrier group.

To Larry, the enemy ships looked like beetles unrolling long white trails on the blue sea, for the dive bombers came in high. The fighters were ahead; Larry saw a few Japanese fighters in the air. The Hellcats went in after them, and Larry saw smoke trail after smoke trail plunging down. Then he turned to look over his shoulder, ahead, and saw the big flat-top.

60

Mister Howard pointed one hand at her and began to spiral down.

The Japanese fleet broke up as its units began to take evasive action, every gun on the ships firing at the planes. The dive bombers circled around in leisurely fashion, splitting up to take different ships from different angles. Down below were four carriers, one of them very big; two battleships which had had their rear turrets removed to make room for short flight decks; three cruisers; nine destroyers; and six escort vessels. Each ship was making top speed, circling and zigzagging, while their hundreds of guns speckled the blue sky with black bursts of AA fire.

"No trouble finding one, eh, Larry?" Mister Howard said softly. "Like a whole covey of quail going up at once—we've got to pick one out. That carrier looks good to me. Okay, boy, here we go!"

The experience again, the wild, exhilarating, frightening plunge down, faster than a falling stone, the scream of parted air, the thuds and shakings of AA fire, the pullout! Larry stared hard as the plane swept up into the sky again. The carrier was surrounded by the high splashes of bomb bursts; as Larry watched, he saw two heavy explosions on her flight deck.

"Two hits, Mister Howard!" he cried, switching over to intercom. "Don't know whether they were ours or not, so many bombs were around her."

"Good enough, Larry. I don't believe we're scratched. We'll head for the barn and get another bomb load."

61

Within minutes the wild scene, with its circling ships, the diving, soaring planes, the water crisscrossed and marked with wakes and pocked with explosions, was far behind them. When they were many miles away, Larry could still see the rising column of black smoke behind them.

Ozawa wanted to suck the Third Fleet up to attack him, and he succeeded. He knew something of the immense strength of this fleet. It consisted of ten carriers, six new fast and powerful battleships, six light cruisers, two heavy cruisers and forty destroyers.

Ozawa had almost no planes, and the ten American carriers were equipped with full loads of new, fast planes flown by expert pilots. Air attacks from the American carriers continued to strike at the Japanese all day, concentrating on the carriers. "Get the carriers!" had always been a Third Fleet battle cry. They did so, this day.

The second strike took off at 0822, just as Admiral Halsey was receiving Admiral Sprague's message about Kurita's stunning surprise attack off Samar. His first move was to detach one of the carrier groups, with orders to steam south and render assistance. As this group of carriers received the orders, Sprague's force seemed doomed, almost surrounded by Japanese battleships and cruisers.

Mister Howard gave the plane to Larry for the flight home, and he flew the entire hundred miles—which was very good for him. He was still singing with the exultation of the 5,000-foot dive, and the possible bomb hits on the carrier's deck. But sober thought came to him also at these moments. The plane had pulled out at eight hundred feet, close enough so that the dots on the carrier's decks were not ants, but men. Larry didn't like the thought of killing men; it was better for it to be ants, or the ships themselves, that he killed. But today there had been men, he had seen them. Thousands of men were down there in that frantic fleet, fighting back bravely, suffering the same fear and pain that he, Larry White, suffered, and a hit on one of the ships meant that some of them died.

Larry was glad he could fly the plane. He kept it as steady and smooth as Mister Howard by now. From the first, flying had seemed a natural thing for him to do.

They landed on the *Lexington* at eleven o'clock with Mister Howard back at the stick. Men were standing on the deck's edge, cheering them. Plane handlers hit the plane with even more than the usual snap and ginger, and even before Howard and Larry White could climb down from the cockpit, men were wheeling 500-pound bombs toward them, while others prepared for fueling, and armorers began to check the still full machine-gun magazines. Larry and the pilot were hustled into Air Control and questioned about what they had seen. An air of burning excitement hung over the ship. Even the dullest of men realized that this was the beginning of the end. The last Japanese carriers were being pounded to bits!

Larry and Mister Howard took off again; at 1300, one o'clock, they were over the enemy fleet. It had suffered a great deal; its cripples were strung back for thirty miles. Two carriers were down, a destroyer had been sunk and the rest of the ships badly hurt, except for the two converted battleships, which were very tough, very fast and very heavily armored. Their anti-aircraft threw up an umbrella of intense fire that made the American pilots wary of too close an approach. Their commanders were apparently experts at avoiding torpedoes, for the fading white streaks of fish tracks intercrossed behind each of them. Vessels burned here and there, and others streamed oil behind them. Their guns were operating, and the dots on their decks were ants now to Larry.

Two hundred planes were in the air, hitting the fleet. The strike force from the *Lexington* concentrated on the big carrier *Zuikakao*. Torpedo planes bored in from the bow, eight hundred feet high, ring-tailed fish ready. The dive bombers came in from the port and starboard bow, port and starboard stern. They came in deliberately, carefully and together.

This time Mister Howard went so low, so straight, in spite of the bucketing AA fire, that Larry actually saw the two black specks that were their bombs arch through the air and strike home on the *Zuikakao*'s decks. At almost the same moment, he saw the high white pillars of three torpedo hits. Then gravity and blackness overcame him; at length he floated back down onto his seat again and peered over the now level cockpit. Both carriers were burning heavily, and the *Zuikakao* was beginning to settle.

"We sure as the dickens got one that time, Mister Howard!" Larry said into the intercom.

"You mean it? You really mean it?"

64

"Two hits, sir. We were the only ones diving from port right then, and I actually saw the two bombs fall and hit her, just aft of the island, a little to the starboard side."

"Wow! Wonderful!" Obviously to Mister Howard these dots were at this moment ants. Larry was happy, but he also wished that Mister Howard would let him fly the plane home.

Mister Howard did. They reached the *Lexington* right on schedule, and as soon as he was out of the cockpit, Mister Howard ran straight for the ladder and tore up it to the admiral's bridge, shouting as he ran, "I got a hit on a carrier, I got a hit on a carrier!"

Larry was surrounded by jubilant crewmen. He felt a little dazed, a little insulated from it all. Still before his eyes was the tapestry of sea, blue, silver, white, ornamented by flame and the curling wakes of vessels. This was his part, his true, real personal part, in one of the great climactic events in man's history. He felt totally apart from these men in this moment.

They didn't fly. He did. Would he ever again ride a dive bomber against a Japanese carrier? Would he ever again play a high part in war's flashing drama of life and death? War was bad, bitter, miserable, he knew, but somehow from a plane in the air fighting against equal foes—other ships, other planes— it seemed less murder than drama. Really, Larry didn't care whether he ever rode into battle again, but he still felt sad when he found that his dive bomber would not be included in the final strike of the day. He felt tired now, drained. He was ready for something to eat, and maybe even some sleep.

65

The sunset of this October 25, 1944, was the sunset for the carriers of the Rising Sun of Japan. When Ozawa's torn fleet finally dispersed into the shelter of the night, all four of his carriers and one destroyer had been sunk, and most of the rest of his force was badly damaged. Trying to escape back to Japan, ship after ship met its fate from pursuing American planes or submarines.

FIVE

SURIGAO STRAITS

ON THE EVENING of October 24, Halsey's force was on its way, but geography had thus far kept the surface fleets apart. The land masses of the Philippine Islands separated the American and Japanese navies. Straits and narrows wound among the scattered, thousand islands. San Bernadino Strait and Surigao Strait were doors that led from the Japanese area into Leyte Gulf, crammed with American shipping. As Halsey's fleet steamed northward in the gathering darkness to destroy the Northern Force, three Japanese admirals moved their ships toward these two straits, hoping to slaughter the invasion armada in the gray dawn.

67

The sailors of the Seventh Fleet in Leyte Gulf knew by now that another enemy force had been sighted in the north; but Halsey and the Third Fleet were on their way to take care of those boys—no Japs were going to take the Seventh Fleet from the rear. All they had to worry about was the force heading for the Surigao Straits. The fire support group—old battleships within Leyte Gulf itself, patrolling destroyers in the east at the mouth of the Strait, thirty-nine PT boats patrolling the narrow passage and the waters as far as fifty miles westward —would handle that one.

What they did not know was that the seas at the eastern end of San Bernardino Strait were empty, so that their northern flank was unguarded.

The heat got to Jerry O'Donnell sometimes. At five in the afternoon in the Philippines, with the PT 493 alongside PT Tender *Oyster Bay,* one could have baked a fruitcake or a Boston Irishman below decks. The tender stopped the land breeze; to the west the sun, still high above the distant hills of Leyte, burned on the eyes and skin like a blowtorch. The ice cubes were melting fast in the plastic glass of lemonade he was carrying. He ducked under the shade of the makeshift awning raised on the forecastle of the boat, stretched out and took a deep drink.

"How's the ice holding out?" Jim Rank asked, lazily.

"Half gone." Jerry sighed in relief as the cold liquid sloshed down inside him. The one luxury the PT's possessed was a good refrigerator, run by auxiliary generators when the main

68

engines weren't going. And the lemonade powder was good stuff. Jerry clinked the fast-vanishing ice cubes in the fast vanishing lemonade. A voice echoed from the deck of the tender—a converted steam yacht.

"Now hear this—Chadown—chadown. . . ."

"Drink up, Jerry."

"Why? It'll be horse sausage and beans again."

"Maybe, but the skipper said for everybody to eat a good supper. He expects us to be out all night—and maybe all day tomorrow, too."

Jerry finished his lemonade and set the glass aside. They joined the other members of the PT boat's crew and climbed the jacob's ladder to the tender's deck, where they went aft to the steamy mess room. Before going inside, Jerry turned to look down on the PT 493. His eyes lit up. He still loved the crazy little boats, as all the PT jockeys did.

She was eighty feet long and twenty wide, with a fine, curving forecastle and a bull nose which slanted slightly downward. Her decks were crowded. Two torpedoes and four depth charges on the Green launching racks, a forty-millimeter oerlikon aft, a thirty-seven-millimeter and a twenty-millimeter forward, two twin fifty-caliber machine-gun mounts and a smoke screen generator aft. The radar, shrouded in its plastic covering, hulked like a large bushel basket on the top of the tripod mast. The boat was painted a dirty green. Even sitting still, she seemed to be moving. Jerry shook his head and went into the mess hall, where he found beans, bologna and hot coffee.

69

"Hot coffee!" he grumbled. "In this weather?"

A neighbor drawled: "Twa'nt hot when they brought it in. You should a got up here quicker. Its just heated up by bein' in this place. I heard them flyboys got air-conditioned ready rooms and staterooms on them big carriers. That's life, man. Be a flyboy."

The sun was behind the mountains when the crew of the PT 493 went back aboard their boat. Pipes, cigars and cigarettes were lit; this was a nervous time, waiting for the old man and the dope about the night patrol to come.

Lieutenant (jg) Dick Brown was a thin, short man who looked like a teacher or a musician. He also looked tired, but eager. The executive officer, Ensign Bob Carter, was bigger and more careless. He kept looking away over the expanse of Sogod Bay while the skipper was talking.

"Well, boys, you're going to be able to tell your grandchildren you were in the biggest naval battle ever fought, I think. The flyboys say they have dusted off one big force, and if they're wrong Bill Halsey and the fast carriers and battleships will take care of it. There's another fleet coming down from the north. For us, there are two enemy forces heading for this Surigao Strait we're supposed to hold. That is, Admiral Oldendorf thinks they're heading here, and he's a smart man, almost half as smart as Jerry O'Donnell thinks Jerry O'Donnell is."

"That does it then," said Mr. Carter. "The admiral's bound to be right."

Jake Henry coughed. Jerry cleared his throat and polished his fingernails on his bare chest.

"We've got a guy named Nishimuru for our share. He's bringing us two battleships, a couple of cruisers and about four destroyers. Behind him is another force, two cruisers and six or seven destroyers."

"I want to go home," somebody said, mock mournful.

"All that for us, Skipper?" Jerry asked. He had to say something to stay in character, but his mouth was dry.

"Well, we've got six battleships, a few cruisers and about fifteen destroyers to help us out. But we'll get first helpings. We'll be patrolling the Straits, just southeast of Hibuson Island. We're lucky. Some of the boats will be as far out as Bohol— that's fifty miles out, in enemy waters. We're supposed to spot the enemy, send contact reports and then get in and make torpedo runs. Okay?"

The 493 boat lay in a nest of three with the 490 and the 491, skippered by Lieutenant John McElfresh and Lieutenant Harley Thompson. The three boats would patrol together, with McElfresh in command. As Jerry swung down into the still-baking chart house with the skipper right behind him to check the charts, he heard and felt the motors of the outboard boat— that is, the one beyond the 493—start up. His stomach turned with it. Another whining of starter and gear, explosion, then deep rumble, toned down. He could smell the acrid hundred octane exhaust fumes in here. All around, PT engines were bursting into life.

"There—about eight miles north of the southern tip of

Panaon Island, a mile and a half north of Calingnan Point—across the Straits to just above Tunga Point. Got it? Good. See that you have the bearings and distances all laid out. We'll be needing them."

"Aye, aye." Jerry was sweating. He hoped it was only the heat. But a night action coming up! Thank God for the radar —at least they'd know something was coming before it got them. He'd done night patrols in a PT without radar, and he'd never gotten over the feelings of blindness and claustrophobia, knowing that danger was near, unseen, drawing nearer. He checked the point of departure and the course to the western end of their patrol areas, and went on deck just in time to hear Mr. Brown say, conversationally, "Okay, wind 'em up." Mr. Carter stood up on the back bench and waved his hand, forefinger extended, in a circle. The motor macs back in the engine room were watching. In a moment the first starter whined, the engine started and roared. The boat vibrated. The second motor joined the first; in a moment, the third. Gray smoke puffed back; then the engines idled down.

Mr. McElfresh made a signal toward the 493, both hands lifted, palms up. Men on the 493 took the other boat's lines from the deck cleats and passed them over to the 490's crew. The 490 went ahead gently on the starboard engine, backing down on the port. She twisted in the water; when her bow was pointed out, the backing engine shifted to forward and she went out gently, her exhaust rumbling and gurgling as small waves blocked the vents and fell away. Jerry watched her square stern move out, her muffled underwater exhaust leads making vertical marks on the streaked green of her stern. The smoke generator, looking like a large oxygen flask lying on its side, stood a little above the deck. Above that, forward, the barrel of a thirty-seven-millimeter gun pointed to the sky.

Jerry had the wheel. Dick Brown gestured forward; Mike took the bow line from the 491. The stern line and breast came aboard, and the gentle wind shoved the 493 away from the other boat. No need to twist her. Jerry moved the wing throttles from neutral to ahead and poked the button, hearing the buzzer sound sharply from the engine room aft, warning the motor macs that a gear shift was to be made. The engines took her. Bill Long took the flag and its staff from the socket astern and the radioman ran up the colors on the stubby tripod mast, alongside the radar basket.

The sun was down now, and the western sky was red, with a few black clouds gathering overhead. Away from the tender, the leading boat picked up speed a little. To keep up, Jerry moved the throttles forward until 1200 RPM showed on the tachs. He evened all three carefully to the same speed. Behind came the sound of the 491 casting off and getting underway. Jerry was glad to be busy watching the interval. Shoving off on night patrol always made him feel a little as if he'd swallowed a large cantaloupe.

The PT 490 swung to the right and parallel to Panaon Island for a way, then turned due east through Panaong Strait. It was a lovely time, if a man could clear the fear from his eyes and mind. The jungled shores of Panaon Island on the right and Leyte on the left flung back the roar of the motors.

73

The water was very calm and glassy before being marked by the wake of the boats. A flight of cockatoos soared up from Panaon, white flecks against the green cliff of jungle. Beach sand was white beneath the trees, and the smell of the tropical islands drifted out to the PT men. The skipper lit a cigar, blew a puff of smoke and looked up at the sky, where red was fading to pink and gold.

"Well, Jerry," he said. "Here goes another one. But it's not barges we're busting tonight. Battleships."

"Maybe we won't have to go as close, Skipper."

"I hope not. Remember the night we scraped paint off the bow rubbing alongside that troop barge?"

"Yes, sir."

Dick Brown fell silent. Another section of PT's coursed the water off to starboard. Jerry watched them, so graceful in motion in the calm water. The tall whip antennas bent backward with the forward motion, and white water was flung up from the bows. That section was going further up the coast of Leyte for patrol.

Full dusk had set in when the 493 reached her patrol station. The three boats fell into a vee formation, a hundred yards apart, and commenced the first eastward beat of the night's patrol. To the northwest dark clouds were mounting, but above them the first few stars were beginning to show.

The skipper relieved Jerry at the wheel, and the latter went below to check the chart and position. They had a fifteen-mile patrol leg, and he figured that in twenty minutes they would come about and take up the westward leg, back to their starting point. He passed the word up the hatchway and swung into the radioman's blue leather chair alongside the hatchway into the chart room, close by the radio set. Beyond the radio was the SC radar and the scope, with Rank bent over it.

The two oblong parts were blacked out now and, with the door to the cockpit open, only a very dim blue light shone above the chart table. The boat was blacked out; unless the doorway was closed, Jerry would use a dim flashlight for chart-work. He stared about the small space, all of it as familiar to him as his own hand. From the door a vertical ladder led on below to the passageway from crew's dayroom to the forward crew's quarters. Officers' quarters, two small cabins, were to port, a soda booth wardroom to the right. It was never used as such aboard; in a PT boat officers and men ate together at the mess table forward. The chart room was neat and clean— Jerry kept it that way. Thompson submachine guns and riot guns hung on the bulkheads, with ammunition belts beneath them. Ranks of chart drawers were beneath the chart table. Three men might stand comfortably in the space; for more it would be crowded. After a little while, Jerry went back up into the cockpit, hating the sour taste of fear in his mouth, but knowing by now that he would do what he had to do when the time came.

By nine o'clock, clouds covered the sky. By nine-thirty, it was beginning to rain. Jerry got into his foul-weather jacket; if a guy got wet out here at night he could get cold, tropics or no tropics. A few messages had passed between boats and they had heard some chatter from other sections, but in general the PT's kept good radio discipline when action was expected. Any message could easily be a matter of life and death.

As the rain came down a wind arose, whipping the waters of the gulf into short, mean whitecaps. The boat rolled and pitched; spray flew over the cockpit occasionally when she stuck her bullnose into a wave. Visibility was zero. Jerry was infinitely thankful for the radar. He went below and checked the radarscope. The boat was shown at the center of the round screen, and the pencil of green light, as it revolved with the antenna above, cut green glows and marks into the screen. They were three miles from Dingebat, on the eastward leg again. Jerry could make out the three boats of the next patrol south, thrashing westward. To the north, on the rim, were many blips, dissolving, returning, moving. They were waiting gunfire and bombardment forces, battleships, cruisers, and destroyers. The islands themselves stood out well on the scope, and Jerry had no trouble keeping a constant true position for the PT. He went back on deck.

Midnight. Earlier the men not directly engaged with duties had, by permission, curled up on the deck in the wet, in a few cases even below, for a wink of sleep. Now, with the danger hour approaching fast, all hands were awake and at battle stations, sleeves rolled down, helmets and lifejackets on, .45's and shark knives at their belts.

Ten minutes after midnight. The night was black, cold, full of fear and suspense. Static was constant on the radio; then voices began to be heard through it. Contact report!

Section One, nearly fifty miles to the westward, had sighted the enemy and attacked. Battleships, cruisers and destroyers. The boats had been caught in searchlights, bracketed by shell fire and driven away after launching torpedoes. PT 130 and PT 152 were hit by 4.7-inch shells, but they survived. They had been unable to radio the contact report, and the 131 had raced full speed to the next section of waiting PT's, whence the report was relayed.

"Twenty-two fifty-four!" the skipper said, quietly. "Then they sighted them over an hour ago. The Japs are making twenty-two knots. We've got an hour to wait, boys."

"I'm not in any hurry," Jerry said, trying to laugh. "Maybe I'll go below and sack out."

"Yes, you do that," the skipper said. "Better off without O'Donnell up here anyway. Nutty Irishman."

"Shh," Bob Carter said. "You'll hurt Jerry's feelings."

Jerry grinned, and he heard Lacey chuckle. Jerry knew that he could have made any crack within reason without objection from the two officers, but he couldn't think of anything appropriate. For a wild moment he was really tempted by the thought of the dark below, of his bunk, of hiding his head under the bedclothes as he had in bed, in the dark, when he was a kid. But a man couldn't hide from what was coming toward them now.

Time dragged by, then moved wildly. Panaon Island screened them from direct vision southwest, but they saw the intermittent blurs of searchlights in the sky, saw the red tinge of firing and heard the distant concussions. The battle

77

was coming nearer. Excited talk surged and flowed over the radio, wild snatches—"Look out, look behind you, Jack!" "There's another one." "Don't run me down, Bill—look at that battleship!" "I don't. . . ." "Come alongside, Jake, for Christ's sake! Dellinger's dying, and Martin's bad hurt. Where's Doc Lastreto? What boat's he on? We got two engines conked out and two feet of water in the engine room. Come alongside, and. . . ."

"There they are! There they are! Jesus, Mary, Joseph be . . . Whaaam!" Indescribable shattering, and blankness.

". . . off Cape Dang . . . God, look at her burn, and . . ." "Section Nine, this is Leeson, Section Six. Mac, we're attacking. They're heading for. . . ."

A crescendo of noise. Jerry gripped his guts with his mind, bit his tongue, held fast. Just minutes, now; the enemy force was sweeping toward them, bound to be. Searchlights snapped on and off not far away; he saw red tracers beading the sky, slow-moving. Then the radarman stuck his head through the cockpit door.

"Skipper! Contact! Four strange radar pips, just rounding south end, Panaon Island. Bandits. No IFF."

"Right." Just then came McElfresh's voice over the radio. "Section Nine, this Nine Boss. Come to course 160, speed fifteen. Mufflers on until you fire. No shooting until you get your fish off. Let's go."

"Come right, Jerry," Mr. Brown said, quietly. "Mike, get impulse charges in the tubes. Bob, unlock firing circuits.

Get helmets on everybody. Gunners, don't fire unless a search-light gets us or I order you to open up."

Jerry realized that the other two boats must have turned sooner or were making more rpm's. The 493 was a couple of hundred yards behind them; he could barely make out the green blur of their wakes.

"Shall I goose her a little, Skipper?" he asked, his hands on the throttles.

"Nope, not if we don't drop further back. Don't want any phosphorescence tonight. Lord! Here's the rain again."

An agony followed for Jerry—suspense, fear, terrible im-aginings—what it must feel like to have a leg blown off, to be eaten, wounded, in the water by sharks. Sweat mingled with the rain on his face.

The rain lifted. Now the 493 was a hundred yards astern of the 490 and the 491. Jerry saw the other PT's first, then beyond them four black shapes on the water. He gasped. The radarman stuck his head out the hatch.

"Seven hundred yards, Skipper!" he grated, his voice shaking. "Jeez, sir, you wanna get trampled like Mr. Kennedy did?"

"Mac hasn't fired yet; we can't fire until he does. Keep her steady, Jerry. Bob, you got the setup on the director?"

"Roger. If their speed is twenty-two and ours is fifteen, and the fish make thirty-six, we've got the leading one for sure. Good angle on the bow."

"Oh, ain't McElfresh *ever* gonna shoot!" the radioman moaned. "He want to hang on to the tail end of the fish and poke it against that Jap cruiser thataway?"

79

Darkness had lifted as the rain squall blew over; now the stealing black shapes so near took on sharply and clearly the lines of four warships, dark, still quiet. Jerry could see the white water at their bows.

He heard the skipper's sibilant sigh. Then "Mac's fired two fish! Lined up, Bob?"

Jerry had seen the high white splash as the 3,000-pound torpedoes dropped into the water from the PT racks, engines already beginning a scream. He tensed; suddenly a mile and a half to the south a searchlight snapped on, its great beam spread wide to encompass the PT's and the enemy ships. The fish wakes moved ahead; 490 started to turn away, Mr. Brown gave the order, "Fire fish! Fire one! Fire two!" The 491 dropped two torpedoes in the water, and then the leading ship of the Jap column turned on a searchlight that caught the three PT's in a straining group, green hulls glistening, white wakes shining. Two more torpedoes hit the water from 490; Jerry, holding the course steady with all his resolution, felt the 493 lurch twice, saw her torpedoes hit the water.

"Right, hard right!" the skipper cried.

More searchlights. Instantly, from the 493 and the other boats began the hard hammering of thirty-seven millimeters, the coughing of forties, the purr of twenties and the rhythmic chugchug of the quadruple fifty calibers. Streams and bursts of tracer hovered in the air. The 493 was turning away. Her smokescreen generator was on. Red blossoms of fire bloomed along the Jap line, and freight trains rumbled overhead and to the side, with high white columns rising as the 4.7-inch shells hit the water. In the hideous sudden noise—straining rising motors, crash, roar, pound, shout—Jerry felt he was standing in silence, except for the rush of his own blood, the pounding of his heart. Tracers floated with deadly slowness in the sky, like red baseballs in line, seemed to bore for his eyes, went overhead. Explosions of small shells flashed aboard the Japs as PT fire went home. Searchlight after searchlight dimmed out. But others were on. Jerry saw fragments fly from a center of red fire on the bow of the 490; then its bow gun was gone, and the boat was rocking and tumbling.

"Four-Ninety's hit!" Brown shouted, shoving the throttles against their forward rests. Make smoke! Jerry, hide her! Quick!"

The 493 bucked up and flung herself across the water, pounding over the crazy combination of wind, wave and wakes, throwing herself out of the water, lunging, smashing down, lunging again, dragging behind her the intense white funnel of chemical smoke. Jerry twisted the wheel, aimed for 490, aimed for between her and the enemy. Another searchlight went off; another came on. More red blossoms and tearing overhead. The air was full of ghostly, metallic noises.

The rising curtain of smoke rose behind the speeding PT, rose alongside the 490, absorbed the searchlight beams, hiding the wounded boat. But the 493, her wake high and dramatic, was too easily seen by the enemy.

There was a whirlpool of shell explosions, tracer, shouting. The 493 rose from the water, dashed sideways, while wood and metal screamed. Jerry, staggering, saw a splash alongside.

A 4.7 shell had torn clear through the boat above the water line. Another smashed into the stern; wood split, splinters flew, a man screamed. The roaring motors coughed, hesitated, slowed, roared again, fired unevenly, the boat's bow dropping. Then Jerry was enveloped in a wall of red and black, mostly red, filled with strange noises, smells and feelings. Hammers hit him, threw him, slashed him. . . .

He woke up stretched over the dayroom canopy. His face was wet and sticky. A blackened form, Bob Carter, he saw in searchlight and fire, was holding one arm stiffly. Jerry's face hurt, his leg hurt. He saw Mr. Carter stagger to his feet and move forward. Jerry tried to follow. He was dizzy and dazed, but he succeeded. The 493's own smoke had caught up with her, blown by a small breeze, and she was enveloped in a saving cloud, through which the diffused light of battle shed a considerable glow. Jerry lurched behind Mr. Carter to the cockpit! Cockpit! Half a cockpit! A shell had taken away the chart room, downed the mast and twisted and bent the light armor plate around the cockpit. Everything smelled of sulfur and death and heat. The wheel was swinging idly, though the engines still ran, unevenly. Mr. Carter took the wheel and turned the bow of the PT away from the blaze and glare beyond the smoke that marked the enemy force. Jerry, sick, saw the radioman lying dead on the deck of the cockpit, a black pool around him.

"God!" he muttered. "God, oh God, oh God!"

The boat was moving steadily now, a good ten or twelve knots, though the tachs were too shattered to read. Keeping the smoke between him and the enemy, Bob Carter pulled her away, out of the fight. Jerry looked back and saw behind him the searchlights fade off, turned off. The firing ceased. He gulped, and then prayed.

"Go back to the engine room and see what the score is," Carter said. "Hey, here's the skipper! Lord, Dick, you've got blood all over your face!'

"So've you ... And Jerry ... Something hit my head. Lord, it aches. Where ... I get it ... where are the other boats?"

Jerry was moving aft. His step was uncertain, but he went from handhold to handhold across the bucking deck. He reached the engine room hatch and looked below.

Light glinted back from sloshing water. One of the machinist's mates lay face downward in it, dead. Another, blood covering one side of his face, was bending over the starboard engine. Al Brunelle was in the seat, his eyes on the gauges. He saw Jerry and tried to smile at him.

Jerry swung down beside him. The clatter was deafening, as it always was.

"What's the dope?" he shouted.

"Smokey's dead, Al's hurt, but he's working on the starboard engine. We got a shell back here, right through." He gulped. Jerry looked in the direction of his gaze and saw cloth at the edge of the water and the white of splintered wood.

"I shoved my life jacket in the hole, and the water isn't rising so fast right now. I think we can keep running for another twenty minutes. Tell the skipper!"

Jerry clapped him on the back and climbed back topside.

His face and leg were hurting more now, but he hardly limped as he walked. Clipped by small splinters or fragments, he guessed. They'd keep. He knew he wasn't bleeding much, or he'd feel weak. He reported to the battered skipper and exec in the remains of the cockpit.

"We're heading for Panaon Island, to beach," Brown said. "Twenty minutes? We'll make it then. Jerry, go collect all the able-bodied men. We want to get the dead and wounded ashore when we hit. I want water, food, blankets and the first-aid kit. Bob and I have morphine syrettes. We'll use them on the beach, after we've looked the boys over."

"Aye, aye sir."

"Take the Thompsons and the riot guns too, with ammunition. All hands keep their .45's. Can't tell around here."

Brunelle had turned on the mufflers again, and the wounded PT slipped through the water with only a quiet throbbing to mark her passage. Radio and radar were gone; no way of telling of their plight, but Jerry knew this was friendly territory —that is, if the battle went right—and that they'd be picked up soon.

If the battle went right.

If it went wrong? That didn't bear thinking of.

Panaon Island was a black wall rising above them. The beach was white in the darkness, with a long necklace of surf. Jerry headed for it, the boat barely moving now. All was strangely quiet, accentuated by the distant fumble of gunfire up the bay, the glow of guns; gunfire about three miles away as the next section of PT's tried its luck. A bird, or a monkey, was crying in the black jungle, and Jerry could smell the shore.

It took resolution to drive the PT on the beach; for many months this idea had been a nightmare to Jerry. The 493 hit slowly, lurched, moved on, stopped and listed to starboard. Dry sand was beneath the droop of the bullnose.

"Abandon ship," Brown said, wearily. "Maybe we can salvage her tomorrow." They could feel the boat settling slowly beneath them, the stern dropping inch by inch as the water gained.

They lowered the two dead men tenderly to the sand. The wounded were next, the seriously hurt in blankets; Jerry, the skipper and Mr. Carter were able to handle themselves. When Jerry's feet hit the dry sand, his knees buckled for a moment. He felt as if he wanted to kneel down and kiss the earth, thinking of the sharks in the dark water.

"Got the water?" Mr. Brown asked. "There'll be some inland if we look, but I want to be sure we have enough here for a while."

"We've got thirteen full canteens, Skipper," Jerry said.

"Cover Smith and Hedges. Poor guys—God rest 'em. Now, anybody want morphine? Are you hurting so bad you can't stand it? Mr. Carter and I have ten shots of it."

The lightly wounded refused; two men, one badly burned by shell flash, the other with a badly ripped leg, took the soothing drug. Those who wished it were laid carefully in the blankets on the sand. Everybody had a drink of water, and cigarettes were passed around. The cook had brought a case of

85

K rations—they would have enough to eat for a couple of days, if necessary.

Violence was growing to the northeast. Jerry's face and leg felt stiff, but not very painful, and he was dying to see what was going on.

"Skipper," he said, "can I climb the rocks? I want to see what happens when the Japs hit the battleships."

"Yes," said Mr. Brown, "and I'm coming with you."

In the end, nine of them climbed a couple of hundred feet up the steep cliff. They paused on a rocky shelf and watched to see the rest of the battle of Surigao Strait unfold.

The Japanese fleet, still relatively untouched after fifty miles of PT opposition, entered the fringes of Leyte Gulf. Here the Japanese admiral's orders had sent him. He had no hope of survival, but here the Japanese Navy would immolate itself, carrying all with it that it could.

Beyond PT's they met destroyers, knifing in on their flanks in the dark, launching torpedoes in fours, sixes, dozens. The enemy force's order was this: four destroyers, then battleship *Yamashiro;* at one-kilometer intervals followed battleship *Fuso* and cruiser *Mogami.* By any normal tactical consideration, this was an ill-balanced force, but in this suicide of the Japanese fleet, the destroyers were not available to make up the proper balance.

Jerry's watch was intact, and its dial glowed softly. At 0256, he saw great horizontal searchlight beams to the north. The last PT's had been passed, frail wooden motorboats fighting 40,000-ton battleships with armor eighteen inches thick and sixteen-inch main batteries. Now the giants would encounter giants—but first, destroyers.

At 0258, Jerry saw the bright glare of star shell in the sky, and in its white illumination he saw, distantly, the lean shapes of destroyers and the massive bulk of the Japanese column. Heavy firing commenced; he could see the tracers soaring and the red hot sparks of larger shells arching into the sky. The Japanese were using flashless powder; their firing showed as quick, red glimmers. A searchlight went off, another came on. Smoke rimmed the horizon in the searchlight and star shell illumination. Then Jerry could see the destroyers retiring. They'd fired their fish, and were going away.

He saw the red and black explosions beginning to rise in the enemy column. Now ships were burning; in the red glare Jerry saw one ship sinking, stern first. It looked like a destroyer.

"Wow!" he shouted. "They're giving 'em hell! Hit 'em, cans, hit 'em!"

A green flare came floating down from the sky toward Leyte. More star shells soared up, the white, great flares hanging, swinging in their parachutes, coming down, illuminating the sea and the dark islands, the ships, the shell spouts. Jerry shouted, hardly hearing himself above the pulsing rumble from the north.

More gunfire, more lean shapes flashing in and out of smoke in the starshell beams. Then great balls of red fire drifted upward as a ship exploded. Jerry's breath left him; in the darkness to the north, split by light, reddened by fire, all the

worst in the creation of man seemed to be striving—fire, blackness, smoke, explosion, the innocent water reflecting, doubling
the gleams. He saw ships break in two, explode, burn. Then
a thunder that drowned all he had ever imagined as the American battle line and flank cruisers, six miles beyond the Japanese,
opened fire. The horizon was a leaping mass of glare and flame.
The American vessels were steaming a course perpendicular
to the line of the Japanese force—the classic crossing of the T.
And had Jerry known it, he was witnessing perhaps the last
time in the world that battleships would cross the T of battleships, and that a fight of major proportions would be settled
by surface gunfire.

The Japanese vessels, firing back with great rapidity and
discipline, were enveloped. The force dissolved, ships winking
right and left. The American fire poured on; Japanese destroyers, cruisers and even battleships tried to retire. The fourteen-
and sixteen- and eight-inch shells shredded them, set them
afire, tore them apart and turned them into blazing, sinking
wrecks.

Nishimuru was destroyed; a little later Admiral Shima's
smaller force came in. PT 137 planted a torpedo amidships in
light cruiser *Abukumu;* it crippled her and aircraft sank her
the next day. The remaining two heavy cruisers and two
destroyers came in as far as the blazing remnants of *Fuso,* then
retired to plan further action. On the way one of the cruisers,
the *Machi,* collided with Nishimuru's surviving cruiser, the
Mogami. The former was badly damaged; after the beating
she had taken, *Mogami* hardly realized she had been hit.

Jerry O'Donnell, standing on his rock on Panaon Island, felt a little sick and very tired. He was hardly elated, though it was evident that the American Navy had won a great victory.

"That finishes it, I guess," Mr. Brown said, easing his injured shoulder in its sling. "Well, they'll pick us up in the morning."

PT 491 did so at dawn; coasting the island, looking for survivors, she saw the 493 and came nosing in. The dead, wounded and weary unhurt of the 493 were taken aboard. The 491 was just easing away from the beach when the remains of the 493, lifted by the high tide, slid off the rocks. With a surge of bubbles and an almost human groan, the PT slid slowly under the sea and was gone. Jerry felt like crying as he watched her.

By five in the morning of October 25, the Japanese southern force was dead. The survivors, Shima's destroyers and two cruisers, were beating it for home. The destroyer *Shiguri* was the only ship of Nishimuru's force that eventually escaped.

One more stage of the battle was done. Score: Americans—one PT boat lost, one destroyer badly damaged; Japanese—two battleships, three cruisers and five destroyers sunk.

The Imperial Japanese Navy had taken a large step toward harikari—an honorable death.

Sunrise, and an hour after. Quartermaster 2/c Jerry O'Donnell lay asleep in the sickbay of the PT tender *Oyster Bay*. His wounds, not serious, had been dressed and stitched; a shot of morphine, a pair of sulfa pills and exhaustion had put him under. He slept soundly in the quiet heat, not knowing that a hundred and fifty miles to the northeast his friends Tom Bellido and Einar Andersen were on the knife edge of death in the next phase of the battle a thousand miles wide. He tossed a little and moaned in his sleep.

Far away the guns still roared and men still died.

SIX

THE UNGUARDED DOOR

IN SURIGAO STRAIT, the flame of burning ships had long been quenched by salt water. The American vessels had gone from General Quarters to Condition Three—half their crews asleep while the others kept watch, threw brass overboard and tended the boilers, engine rooms and bridge, not yet fully realizing the magnitude of the events through which they had labored and fought.

The first glimmer of dawn appeared in the east—a strip of pale gray just above the heaving horizon of the ocean. Men on watch felt wearier, knowing that relief was not far off.

They had another cup of coffee; lookouts wiped weary eyes and put the night glasses to them again. The quiet bridges seemed tired, but the grooved routine of the Navy moved on. Cooks and bakers already were up, still weary from passing ammunition during the battle, but ready now for a more prosaic task—the feeding of hungry men.

Far to the north, Halsey and the Third Fleet were awake. Just now, search planes were surging forth from the carrier decks to hunt for Ozawa and the last carriers of Japan. Admiral Halsey, his decision made, hoped for the annihilation of the enemy fleet he had risked so much to find.

And at dawn, Admiral Kurita and his Center Force, having passed through San Bernardino Strait unmolested, were only a few miles north of the Task Force of escort carriers moving back and forth in their prescribed tracks. On their decks waited torpedo bombers and fighters, armed, checked, fueled and ready for the day's task of supporting the Army ashore, of searches, of anti-submarine patrol. Busy ships they were; rather humble ships, in a way. The queenly fast carriers of the Third Fleet sought the mighty enemy where he coursed on the ocean and attacked him. The escort carriers, converted merchantmen or Kaiser-built cargo ships finished off as carriers, wove their prosaic ways through the Pacific, ferrying planes, furnishing air cover for convoys, making floating airfields for invasion forces that had not yet won their air strips ashore. Work horses. Their pilots landed on tiny decks that heaved and pitched in a way the great carriers did not; they slept in cabins with temperatures of 98 or above; they waited in non-air-conditioned ready rooms with the mercury hitting one hundred. They received few medals. But they served.

Tom Bellido had the midwatch as gun captain of the *Gambier Bay*'s lone five-inch gun. That means that at 1145 he approached the dim metallic gleam of the gun and said, "Smitty?"

"Right here, Tom. Mighty glad to see you, boy."

"Ready for the sack, huh? Well, here I am. Any orders?"

"Nope, just keep your eyes peeled in case a submarine tries to run up our stern. Request permission to open fire if there's time; otherwise, use your own discretion. That's what the OD told us when we come on watch."

"Okay. Everybody here?" The muster was complete—Tom, pointer, trainer, first shellman, second shellman, first and second loader. Ammunition was in the ready box. Tom checked his men and saw that all of them wore helmets and kapok life jackets.

"Okay, Smitty, go hit the sack. See you at GQ, man."

Another watch beginning. Some stars were in the sky, but a squall off to starboard was sending a thin sheet of warm rain over the *Gambier Bay*. *Kitkun Bay* was a large black bulk off to starboard, soundless, lightless, vague in outline, not showing any sign of the eight hundred men who lived, slept and worked aboard her. Like a floating island in the night, laden with human cargo, high-octane gas, torpedoes, bombs, bullets—and dreams.

"Hey, Tom," said Mike, the pointer. "How didja make out in the poker game?"

"Didn't play."

"You let Wajinski, the crazy Pole, scare you off? Well, it figures. Us Poles are pretty hard to lick—huh, Ladley?"

"Poles, hah," Tom said, grinning, beginning to wake up. "I just didn't want to take his money. Okay, guys, a little bull shooting is fine, and in a little while I'll send somebody to the gallery for some coffee, but I want three men watching that horizon all the time—*all* the time." His hand moved down to the primers in the canvas belt at his waist. The second loader was talker on watch; Tom checked with him to see that the line to the bridge talker was clear and ready. All was well. Tom moved to the aft end of the gun tub and looked out at the dark sea. He was wishing he'd got up a bit earlier and had had time for a cup of coffee at the galley. In a little while he'd send one of the men, but it didn't do to do this too soon. A man needed something to break up the watch, and twice was about all the coffee run that could be made during a watch.

The watch was a quiet one. Little sound was to be heard aboard, except for an occasional clatter from the hangar deck forward and the small talk and muffled noise as a readied fighter or bomber was taken up on the elevator to be spotted on deck for the morning operations. Tom's carrier group was known as Taffy Three. He knew that two more similar groups of escort carriers, Taffy One and Taffy Two, were operating to the south—Taffy Two off the entrance to Leyte Gulf, Taffy One just north of Mindanao.

He thought then of the enemy force to the north, the one with carriers in it. But the Third Fleet was off that way, and

Halsey would take care of it. And the one called Center Force —Larry White and the rest of the flyboys had turned that one back. But Tom felt vaguely uneasy. He had seen enough of the Japanese Navy to know that it didn't turn back very easily. Well, hell. He looked up at the lip of the flight deck above his head, cutting off the sky forward. The old *Gambier Bay* had a few marbles herself—a dozen torpedo bombers, a dozen fighters and five dive bombers. The torpedo planes were being bomb loaded for anti-submarine work and troop support ashore. Together, the six escort carriers of this group could send a swarm of planes buzzing like hornets around an enemy.

Time moved by. Tom watched carefully, kept his crew alert and reported every half hour to the OD on the bridge. At night, when the planes didn't fly, this gun was the only defense the escort carrier possessed. She had plenty of forty- and twenty-millimeter AA guns, but this five-inch thirty-eight was the only thing that could send a surfaced submarine stalker below so that the *Gambier Bay* could run away from him, at her top speed of seventeen knots. So Tom and his men and the lookouts about the ship watched mostly the dim and heaving sea. Coffee came from the galley; hands curved lovingly about the heavy mugs.

"Glad God made coffee when he made the world," Ennis said once. "Don't know how I'd get through the midwatch otherwise."

Night was at its blackest when Tom turned over the watch to another gunner's mate and went below to the compartment. Nearly four o'clock. If he hurried, he'd have an hour and a half to sleep before dawn General Quarters and Flight Stations. He slid into the bunk with the wonderfully luxurious feeling of another watch done—hundreds behind him, hundreds ahead, if he was lucky, but this one was done. He slept.

Dawn now. The gray streak was wide, building upward. The thicker darkness vanished, and suddenly the ocean was no longer a carpet of black; it had white-capped waves in it and showed gradients of color. Stars faded. A dim blur to the west became a distant island. Then, at once, light was full, hard and gray over the ships, and the alarm gong and the boatswain's pipes called tired men from sleep to the new day beginning.

Tom was at his post again with the dawn. He cowered beneath the thunder as the morning flights took off—bombers to hit airfields, to pursue Nishimuru's survivors, to search for submarines; fighters to fly combat air patrol over the carriers. When night was gone and day rose clear and cool over the sea, the *Gambier Bay* secured from General Quarters and Flight Quarters. Condition Three was set, and most of the officers and men went below for breakfast. The *Gambier Bay* served good food. Tom sat down at the mess table and looked over his breakfast tray with pleasure. Grapefruit chunks, eggs, bacon, hashed potatoes, coffee, milk, doughnuts.

"Man, that Bellido can put it away," Ennis said, grinning.

"I don't notice you starving, Bud," Tom said, putting down his fork and reaching for the coffee pitcher. He was thinking that about half the morning should be spent at the five-inch, checking the block and air, maybe even bore-sighting her. But probably that could wait. Anyway, by about ten-thirty he might be able to get an hour's sleep. The midwatch left a man a little short.

In the tremendous arena of this battle, action that had slowed for darkness began to pick up. Army troops ashore began to shove ahead; planes from the Taffys moved ahead of them, hitting bridges and concentrations. Other planes went after the now distant survivors from Nishimuru's and Shima's forces. Well to the north of Leyte, the fast carrier groups of the Third Fleet began to launch strikes in anticipation of the expected sighting of Ozawa. Eager commanders orbited their planes fifty miles north of the fleet, to be closer to the enemy when the word arrived.

Off Samar, Taffy Three ploughed peacefully over the blue water with Samar a faint blue haze to the westward. The routine plane flights had been launched. The destroyers and destroyer escorts of the plane guard force and screen hovered around them, pinging for possible submarines, with lookouts alert for any stray Japanese planes. Combat air patrol buzzed sleepily overhead. Search planes were moving west.

To the northwest of this carrier force, not more than thirty miles away, a major Japanese fleet ploughed along, heading for Leyte Gulf. Its track took it squarely toward the escort carriers. One of the anti-submarine patrol bombers from Taffy Three saw the shapes through the rain squalls that marched this damp, rainy sea in random succession, leaving clear spaces with blue sky, then damping down again with grayness and

97

rain. The pilot was surprised. He thought that Halsey and the Third Fleet were further away than this. He began to count. Ten or twelve destroyers, five or six cruisers and, by God, four battleships. Didn't look like the new ones—the masts looked almost like tall pagodas. He turned his plane in that direction to check.

Tom Bellido was sent up to the after-bridge mount of twenty millimeters—one of the guns had jammed in practice firing the day before, and the recoil spring was cracked. Tom had his tools and a spare spring with him, and he set to work on the gun immediately, with the taste of coffee in his mouth. It was only 6:45; this job wouldn't take long, then he could get to the five-inch and still have time for that nap before the noon meal.

"Lookit over there," one of the two-man twenty-millimeter crew said, idly. "I see some anti-aircraft fire."

"Where?" Tom looked up. "There? Nobody out there to do any shooting. You're . . ." Then Tom too saw the black bursts in the sky, a long way off. The bridge had seen it too. Tom heard feet running, and somebody yelled, "Sir, sir! I hear funny voices on the TBS—They're not talking English, either!"

Cold heaviness began to form in Tom Bellido's stomach. What the devil! Somebody turned up the volume on the TBS on the bridge, and Tom could hear strange, guttural voices. Then an American voice broke in.

"Home Base, this is Outfielder! I'm up over a Jap fleet! Destroyers, battleships, cruisers! They bear three zero zero degrees from you; range, twenty miles!"

A voice said calmly on the bridge: "Tell that pilot to check identification. They must be friendly forces."

Tom heard the reply. "Friendly, hell! They're shooting at me!"

More AA bursts just over the horizon. Tom dropped his tools and stared. Just then a bridge lookout yelled: "Bridge, bridge! I see ships—lots of ships! Looks like Jap battleship masts!"

The air rumbled. Half a mile astern of the *Gambier Bay* red and green splashes rose high into the air!

"We're under fire!" a voice shouted from the bridge; then the General Alarm began its steady clanging. Tom was down the ladder and sprinting across the flight deck before he could really realize what was happening, the unbelievable fact that the carriers were being attacked by a heavy Japanese fleet. Tom flung himself down a ladder from the flight deck to the hangar deck, and ran aft. He came out into sunlight again at the gun mount and hauled open the breech of the gun. The loaders slid in the long brass shell; Tom closed the breech, whipped a primer from the belt that hung ready and inserted it. The gun was ready to fire. But fire! At battleships? Tom had a friend who was a signalman, a job that gave him access to information about much of what was going on outside the *Gambier Bay*. Tom knew that with Halsey somehow vanished, there was no vessel nearer than the gunfire support forces in Leyte Gulf that could handle the Japanese battleships and cruisers. Somebody had busted! Somebody had busted something awful, and Tom knew enough to realize that the American Navy was facing the greatest potential disaster in its history. Let the Japs burst through this flimsy screen of escort carriers, destroyers and destroyer escorts, and it could be in Leyte Gulf within a few hours. Maybe Oldendorf and Fire Support could stand them off, but there would be a slaughter in the transports and auxiliary vessels. The Navy might lose fifteen or sixteen carriers in Taffy Three and Taffy Two, in addition to damage at Leyte Gulf.

On his flagship *Fanshaw Bay,* Rear Admiral Clifton Sprague, USN, commander of Taffy Three, had thoughts more bitter than Tom Bellido's. This could only be the enemy Center Force; it had not turned back and had instead come through San Bernardino Strait. But where was Halsey? A moment's paralyzing fear and despair swept over the man in whose tanned hands lay the fate of six carriers, three destroyers and four destroyer escorts—just the first stake on the table, with uncounted others possibly to follow if he made the wrong move. He knew that the Center Force included the *Yamamoto,* the most powerful battleship in the world, carrying 18.1-inch guns. She alone should be able to handle the old battleships of the distant fire support group. But he had to stop her, somehow, with what he had.

Admiral Sprague had been trained never to give up and to make do with what he had. He squared his shoulders, accepted the burden of the command of what so easily could be a totally destroyed force and gave his orders quickly and calmly. First he looked about again. As no vessel since the days of sail, the carrier is dependent on wind direction for its every decision, for planes must be launched into the wind, or nearly so, and recovered in the same way.

Half an hour after sunrise. A fair day, with cumulus clouds covering one third of the sky. An eight-knot wind, rising to fifteen knots in rain squalls. It blew from east northeast. Smoke lay low and dense in the heavy air. Good. He could head away from the enemy and launch planes. He gave his orders.

Increase speed to sixteen knots. Come to due east. Launch every plane that can fly to attack the enemy. Every vessel make smoke. He then broadcast an urgent message, in plain English, announcing the situation and requesting all assistance possible. The easterly course was taking him further from such help, but he would edge around in a great circle; if the enemy pursued, he could keep him from getting between the carriers and the rest of the American fleet. After five minutes he ordered speed increased from sixteen knots to flank speed—seventeen and a half knots.

The admiral clamped his jaw and settled down on his flag bridge to see what his fate would be. For the moment, it would lie in the hands of his aviators. His eye strayed out to the destroyers and destroyer escorts. Such feeble chips against a 60,000-ton battleship with eighteen-inch guns.

Tom Bellido stood by his gun, which was still useless because of the range, and watched the varicolored shell splashes and the faint smudge on the horizon that was Japanese battleships astern. To him, this was a waking nightmare. Running, when the pursuer could run faster; ready to fight, but knowing that you had no chance against the monster behind you. There was one thing of cheer—the quick-spaced roar and rattle above as plane after plane took off, flashing shapes that dropped, sometimes nearly as far down as his gun platform, and then peeled away into the bright sky. Fear took him, ebbed away and was replaced by a strange sort of exhilaration. Okay, he was dead. They were all dead. No doubt about it. But, by the living God who made men and courage as well as fear, they'd do their level best before the dark closed down. And since death had been brought so close, had become so unavoidable, there was absolutely no use worrying about when it came. So to hell with being afraid!

Einar Andersen yawned—he couldn't help it. True, he had had the second dog watch the evening before (six to eight) and so had had a full night's sleep—that is, until three-thirty this morning. Counting the movie, about six hours. But 6:30 was still early. Sun up, the *Johnston* on course and at proper interval, nothing to do right this moment. Morning star sights already taken and worked out. It had gotten so that sometimes the navigator didn't even get up for the sights anymore.

"Andersen," he had said, the night before. "You're God's gift to a poor navigator. Your positions are as good as mine. Since you're going to be on the bridge anyway, go ahead with the morning star sights. I'll be up before eight for the dope and to check your figures—hah hah. Rank hath its privileges. Good night, my dear Chief Quartermaster."

Einar had realized the compliment behind this. A navigator's professional career might easily hinge on the positions he gave the skipper, and Mr. Jones knew that Einar's navigation was faultless.

Einar was prouder of being a chief quartermaster in the United States Navy, stationed on the USS *Johnston,* than he was of anything else on earth. He'd gone from second class to chief after that night in Kula Gulf—the old man had said it was the best damned job of navigating he'd ever seen, and that he, Ernie Evans, wasn't going to have a seaman like Andersen wasting his time on wheel watches. Anybody who could bring those seven rubber boats off reefs like that, take 'em out to sea and hit the rendezvous on the nose using the stars and a pocket compass, with a bullet through his left arm, ought to be an admiral, but he, Ernie Evans, was only a lousy Cherokee Commander, not a blankety-blank admiral, so all he could do was make Andersen a chief. Okay?

Einar, feeling the calm fulfillment of knowing that he was where he belonged and doing a job he loved, looked about the bridge of the USS *Johnston,* destroyer. Best destroyer in the Navy, and that meant the best ship in the Navy and, as far as Einar was concerned, the best ship in the world.

The captain had chairs in both wings of the bridge—standard equipment, though Commander Evans rarely used the comfortable perches, preferring instead to prowl restlessly about the bridge, cat-like, smoking cigarette after cigarette and keeping a sharp eye on all that went on. At the moment he was asleep in his sea cabin behind the chart house. In front of the chart house was the pilot house; within it were communications equipment, binnacle, wheel, voice tubes, radar scopes. The open bridge spread to either side of the pilot house and across its front, equipped with radar scopes, gyro repeaters, alidades, signal lights, phones, TBS speakers—all the equipment necessary for the men stationed here to control every phase of the destroyer's operations. Above the pilot house was the director, with the radar fire control antenna about it. Just below the bridge forward was the number-two gun, a five-inch thirty-eight in its splinter-proof turret. Seemingly far below were the forecastle, the number-one turret and the thin bow stretching forward. The two wings of the bridge merged into the signal bridge, just aft of the chart room, where the signal gang stood poised and ready to use signal flags or signal searchlights. Einar looked the area over critically. The men didn't stand stiffly as they did during the skipper's or admiral's inspection; they lounged or stood or paced in dungarees, dyed hats and open-necked shirts. But their dungarees were clean and the hats properly squared, and they moved on clean decks beside clean bulkheads. Every item of operating equipment was in good condition, properly cared for and in complete order. The look-outs' eyes never left their sectors, and the signal chief never let his attention wander for more than a second or so from the ocean's rim.

Einar noticed that the signal chief aft was standing like iron at the rail, his long glass steady on something over the sea's edge. Einar frowned; the sea should be empty there. What had Carter spotted? He strolled aft to the signal chief.

"What do you see, Randy? Whales?"

Carter didn't move the long glass, but Einar could see his cheek muscles working over his chew. Randy Carter was an old-time Navy signalman, and his eyes didn't miss anything that eyes could see.

"Whales? No. But by the Mighty, I see something for sure. Yep!" The glass was lowered, and Carter turned to Einar. "You'll say I'm nuts, but I see battleship masts just over the horizon!"

"Third Fleet, I guess, huh?"

"Nope." Carter shook his head. "Masts aren't right. They look like Jap masts to me."

If it had been anybody else, Einar would have laughed. Now sharp coldness flooded through him.

"Let's call the captain—anyway, the OD." Einar ran forward to the officer of the deck, who was standing close by the gyro repeater, where he had been checking bearings of the *Gambier Bay*.

"Something sighted on the signal bridge, sir," Einar said.

"What? Must be something pretty terrific, Andersen. You look pale."

Einar gulped. "Jap battleships, sir."

"It's not April first, is it? You mean it? Hell. Who saw 'em?"

"Randy Carter, sir."

"Carter? Carter saw 'em? That's. . . . I'll call the captain."

"Bridge!" came a cry from above. "Bridge—masthead lookout; I see anti-aircraft fire to the northwest!"

"AA fire? He's nuts!" The OD whirled to look; Einar

strained his eyes. No need. Plainly seen, just above the horizon, were the black bursts of distant anti-aircraft fire.

"Hey!" said the talker. "What's them by the *Gambier Bay?* Whale spouts?"

"They're in technicolor then," someone added, in disbelief.

"Those are Jap battleship main battery salvos!" the OD gasped. "They color them with dye for spotting—Andersen, for God's sake, go call the old man!"

As Einar raced for the chart house door, he heard Admiral Sprague's message announcing the contact and the situation, and making plain the need for help. Then he was in the sea cabin, shaking the sleeping man by the shoulder.

"You're not drunk," said the dark, round-faced man, sitting up in the bunk. "Not you—not Einar Andersen. You mean the Jap fleet is out there, shooting at us? By God! Be right there, son. Sound General Quarters!" As Einar burst out of the doorway, he heard the captain's enraged bellow, "Pants! Where the heck's my pants? Enrico! Enrico!"

In thirty seconds Commander Evans paced out of the chart house. He was walking slowly and sedately. His freshly pressed khakis were spotless, his gold-braided cap square on his bullet head. He was whistling a little tune as he walked.

"Good morning, Lee," he said to the OD, ignoring the tumult of crew and ship hitting battle stations. "Japanese fleet, I believe you said? Well, well. Then I guess we'll earn our pay, gentlemen."

"I guess we will, Captain," said the OD, his pale, strained face relaxing in a smile.

"Let's see. Hmmm. Those are Jap battleships, all right. I guess the *Yamamoto* is one of them, from what I've heard. Yes, shell splashes. Big, aren't they? What are the carriers doing?"

"Launching planes, Skipper," Einar said, a warmth flowing through him.

"Well, Billy Mitchell sank a battleship at anchor, an old one, ready to sink, with no defenses and not moving. Now let's see what the flyboys can do to the live battleships. You know what, Einar? Lee? It's up to us."

"Against eighteen-inch guns, sir?" Lee asked, his face changing.

"They got to hit you with 'em before they can hurt you. We're at General Quarters? Good. Send word to the torpedo officer that he has first innings. Be all set to be all set. We'll make a torpedo attack on that Jap fleet soon, or my name's not Evans. By the Lord! You white men are lucky the Cherokees have forgiven you for what you did to them! I'm going to take that dang blasted *Yamamoto*'s scalp. Sharpen your scalping knives, *Johnstons*," he suddenly yelled. "Old Ernie Evans is doing his war dance, singing his death song! Let's see how many we can take with us!"

Fear was gone from the *Johnston*'s bridge; the boatswain's mate of the watch had held the lever of the PA system down, and the captain's voice had spread over the ship. Warming to the captain's words, Einar heard the cheers being raised fore and aft on the *Johnston,* even though she was, without question, a doomed ship.

In the days of John Paul Jones, a naval force faced by overwhelming odds would have been asked to surrender, been offered life instead of death for the men aboard. In this modern war, parley held no place. No stronger foe would hesitate to sink the weaker; no weaker would expect mercy. The men of Taffy Three, carriers, destroyers and destroyer escorts, accepted these facts of life and death, saw death looking at them and faced death—if not without fear, at least without allowing fear to enter into their calculations and actions.

Within what seemed to be minutes, but what actually was half an hour, Einar could see the hulls of the Japanese forces rising above the horizon. Rain squalls and smoke formed patches of invisibility; the day was dark with smoke, pregnant with danger, the sky now blue, now black, now sunny, now rainy, with great trails of black smoke twisting and twirling over all. A lookout said, "My eyes must be going bad, Chief. I keep seeing black specks all round those Jap battleships."

Einar put his seven-fifties to his eyes. He too had seen the specks, and through the glasses he saw that they were airplanes —fighters, bombers—peeling the length of the enemy vessels, sometimes below the levels of the pagoda masts. He saw bomb spouts rising, he saw the dim flashing of machine-gun fire. All the secondary Japanese batteries were firing at the planes; the main batteries continued with the carrier force, but Einar saw the strafers, the bombers, the fighters, buzzing Japanese decks, twisting about the masts, diving, bombing, machine-gunning. Gulliver and the Lilliputians, maybe, he thought, but they're there, they're buzzing and bombing and launching torpedoes. And pretty soon it will be our turn.

The carriers, the destroyers and the destroyer escorts were making smoke, sending out tumbling black worms from their funnels that expanded into great black clouds sinking low over the hazy sea. The enemy capital ships, cruisers and battleships, screened by destroyers, were drawing up on the quarter of the American force. To the right was Desron 2, its lean ships reaching out to head the cruisers and battleships to port. Then came Cruiser Division 5, *Haguro* and *Chokai,* in column. One kilometer to port of this division was Crudiv 7, composed of heavy cruisers *Kumano, Suzuya, Chimume* and *Tone.* To port of this cruiser division was Destroyer Squadron 10.

Following majestically behind was Battleship Division 1, the *Yamamoto* and *Nagato.* About fifteen hundred yards to their port was Battleship Division 3, composed of the *Kongo* and the *Haruna.*

Battleships and cruisers were firing at the American carriers. As yet their fire was wild, and the American vessels, twisting and turning, reaching for shell spouts, rain squalls and smoke clouds, were unhurt. This could not go on for long. Death and destruction hovered over the sea. Only the most heroic of sacrifices could forestall them.

The sacrifice was ready. *Johnston* and *Hoel* now had all boilers on the line, and all torpedo tubes trained out. They could smell the sacrifice as well as anyone. Though they didn't call it a sacrifice.

SEVEN

DESTROYERS, ATTACK!

No ONE KNOWS what happened to Kurita that day. With methodical deadliness he should have wiped out the American carrier force. But somehow the Japanese seemed as surprised as the Americans, and far more confused. After Admiral Sprague's call for help, planes were taking the air from as far away as Leyte Gulf itself and hurrying to the aid of the escort carriers. Their own planes were attacking the enemy in twos and threes as soon as they were in the air. Torpedo planes dropped their fish, then passed again and again over the enemy capital ships, simulating torpedo runs to keep the Japs firing at them. Fighters strafed enemy bridges and decks; after machine-gun ammunition was used up, the fighter pilots flew "dry runs" across the battleships and cruisers, sometimes below the mastheads.

Kurita, excited at the prospect before him, made a mistake. He issued the order "General Attack," which was interpreted by his command as orders to hit the enemy independently. The force tore for the Americans without coordination or organization, and committed itself piecemeal. The Japanese formation broke up as the various vessels rushed toward the prey before them.

Seeing the enemy in such hot pursuit, Admiral Sprague ordered course changes from time to time, curving the entire running fight around so that eventually it headed toward the southwest, from where help was most likely to come. The eager Japanese kept pace with him, pulling up on the port side of the formation. The American carriers were in a roughly circular disposition, about a thousand yards apart. The destroyers and destroyer escorts were in a ring around the carriers, about six thousand yards from the center of the circle. The Japanese were losing formation as they moved swiftly nearer, firing as they came.

Einar Andersen stood on the *Johnston*'s bridge, life jacket on and helmet in place. He had the quartermaster's glasses at his eyes, and he glanced down now and again at the alidade with its gyro repeater, reading off enemy bearings to Commander Evans.

"Four cruisers hauling up on this side, Captain," he said, trying to make his voice steady.

"Very well." Commander Evans looked aft at the great cloud of black smoke his vessel was dragging behind it. "Don't like making smoke," he growled. "Fouls up the boilers." Then he grinned. "I expect they'll last, though."

"Battleships astern of the carriers are coming closer, Captain," reported the talker, relaying word from the masthead lookout.

"So I see. Boatswain's Mate, pass this word to the crew: 'The *Johnston* is preparing to attack a major portion of the Japanese Fleet. Good luck to you all.'"

Einar heard the shrill sound of the boatswain's pipe over the speakers, followed by the usual harsh, penetrating prelude, "Now hear this!" The captain's message followed; instead of the groan that might have arisen, Einar heard a round of cheers run through the destroyer. Somebody on the starboard forties yelled "Good old G.Q. Johnny!" Einar smiled a little. That's what the men called the ship—G.Q. Johnny—for it seemed to them that this vessel spent all of her time at General Quarters. Her one short year of life had been a busy one, indeed.

"Ten degrees left rudder," Commander Evans ordered. "Come to course 085 True."

"Come left to course 085 True, sir," the helmsman answered from within the pilot house.

Einar gripped the rail hard; the skipper was turning toward the enemy. The *Johnston* was the vessel closest to the approaching Japanese, and Einar knew that the skipper was trying to

make his smoke screen as effective as possible by cutting between the Japs and the desperate carriers.

"What's the range to that leading cruiser, Guns?" Evans
bellowed over the intercom.

"Eighteen thousand yards, sir," the gunnery officer replied
from his position above in the director.

"Open fire, main battery. Salvo fire. Target, leading cruiser
of that column pulling up on our port beam."

A brief pause. Then, "Brranngg!" The destroyer shook and
leaped as her five main battery guns let go at the same instant.
Einar went up on his toes; the blast of Number Two gun,
nearly on a level with the bridge, slapped at him like an angry
hand. The ship rang with the noise of falling brass shells, hiss
of air. "Brranngg!" A second salvo was on its way.

Einar trained his glasses on the leading cruiser, but he
couldn't see the fall of shot. At that moment, several carrier
planes were attacking the column. The ships were half hidden
by the smoke of their AA fire, and shell spouts and bomb
spouts were intermingled. But Einar thought he saw a shell
burst on the forecastle of the leading cruiser.

The planes made a second run; the *Johnston* fired salvo
after salvo, edging out toward the enemy. Andersen saw, astern
of the four leading cruisers, another cruiser with a vast fire
springing up from her stern. One of the torpedo planes must
have laid a thousand-pound bomb on her fantail. Einar cheered.
That one was dropping back already, probably out of this running fight. Looked like she had lost steerage way, at least for
the time being.

Now the planes had finished their runs; the smoke veil rose from about the cruiser. The *Johnston* fired on; Einar saw a series of bright, reddish winks along the sides of the targets— They're firing horizontally! he thought. I wonder. . . .

Trains rushed through the air overhead, and a series of splashes rose into the air three hundred yards beyond the *Johnston*. They were colored purple, Einar noticed; then he remembered his duties, and entered the last course change and the commence firing in the notebook he carried with him. His bearings were all fouled up; no use trying to keep them straight in this day of rain, smoke and terrible danger. Let somebody else worry about the *Johnston*'s track chart today. Would it ever be laid out? Would anybody ever see it?

"To Wolves and Little Wolves, this is Taffy Three." The TBS speaker blared. There was sorrow in the calm voice, or so Einar thought.

"Here we go!" said Commander Evans, rubbing his hands together.

"Wolves and Little Wolves, attack enemy with torpedoes." A pause. "Good luck, gentlemen. And God bless you."

The crew of the *Johnston* received the orders in disciplined silence when the captain repeated them over the PA system. Every man aboard had known it was coming. Einar could judge their feelings only by his own. The thing was so mad, so crazy, that it resolved into plain common sense. By continuing only to run, the American force would be wiped out, carriers, destroyers and all. But if it struck back hard enough, the enemy might be slowed down so that the carriers at least could escape. Or some of them. Einar saw great shell spouts straddle *St. Lo* and *Gambier Bay*. He thought briefly of Tom Bellido, and wished him luck. The planes were raising the devil with the Japs; Einar could see the way the four cruisers to port, and even the battleships astern, were weaving and turning. The water out there must be streaked with torpedo tracks, he thought.

Well, let the destroyers add to them; let the *Johnston* sling ten fish into the water and create still more confusion. Hits would be wonderful; but at the very least the enemy would lose speed and time dodging. The *Johnston?* She was done for anyway. If an early expenditure would buy time so that help could arrive, then it was better to go in now.

"Okay," said Commander Evans, rubbing his hands again. "Torpedo Officer!"

"Fish, aye aye."

"Stand by to fire fish. Torpedo director will take over direction of course and speed. Target, the leading cruiser in that column of four."

"Target, leading cruiser." A pause. "Come to course 047 True."

Commander Evans gave the course to the helm, and turned to Einar.

"This makes it a longer run in under fire, but we'll get a good angle on the bow. Lordy, Lordy! No shortage of targets today. In we go! Full speed!"

The decks began to vibrate more intensely; the stern squatted down and the bow rose, knifing through the seas and creating wings of white spray. The masses of black smoke streamed aft like a dingy banner. Faster and faster the *Johnston* hurled herself through the water.

"Bridge! Skipper! This is the Gunnery Officer. Four hits observed so far on leading cruiser. We've split fire, and hit the second cruiser twice. One hundred rounds expended so far!"

"Good work, Guns! Wish I knew a Cherokee war cry. Keep firing. We're going in for a torpedo run!"

The shallow angle of approach on the Japanese column kept all five guns unmasked, and the Gunnery Officer continued with salvo fire, all guns going off at one touch of the firing key. But also, Einar observed grimly, it put the Japanese cruisers in echelon, relative to the *Johnston,* and unmasked all their batteries as well. Fire winked up and down the cruiser column, no longer sparks, but sudden red glares, like a quick glimpse through an open furnace door. The air was resounding constantly with the tearing, rumbling passage of shells. Spouts were rising before *Johnston,* alongside her, astern of her. Red, yellow, purple, green—the dye showed that they were under fire from a number of ships. Heavier rumblings overhead, then monstrous, varicolored spouts soared into the air beyond the *Johnston.*

"The battleships have joined in," Commander Evans said.

"Bridge!" It was the Gunnery Officer, Lieutenant R. C. Hagen, again. "Shall I switch one gun and take care of that battleship? We might be able to dent her a little."

The skipper of the *Johnston* laughed; to Einar he sounded genuinely amused.

"Ah, let him alone, for now. What's the matter, Guns? Can't you pick on somebody your size?"

"I wish I could. I. . . ."

Rumbling drowned him out; strange hot winds blew across the bridge; then the enormous spouts rose so high and so close that when they collapsed spray rained down on the bridge. Einar found himself laughing too. Madness was contagious; what better thing could a man do than laugh at this mad moment?

The *Johnston* was approaching thirty knots now, heeling sharply every time she changed course. The skipper was calling course changes in to the helmsman, chasing salvos a little—that is, turning toward shell splashes, hoping to make enemy gunners overcorrect. More spray on the bridge, the clatter of fragments on steel decks.

"Heck with this!" cried Evans. "So many salvos I can't chase 'em—and it's slowing us down too much. Back to base course, Helmsman. Andersen! Tell the engineers to squeeze another few knots out of her!"

"Aye aye, sir!" Einar shouted the message over the inter-com—it was quicker than the JV phones.

Choking suspense rose in Einar. Each minute was endless. The *Johnston* was still unhit! How long could miracles last, how long? The enemy column was close now; he could see the individual guns, and every ship was ablaze with gunfire from stem to stern. Aircraft were diving on them, flashing through smoke clouds, rising, engines whining, screaming, bombs exploding. Einar could see even the far distant sparks of tracer and machine-gun fire.

"Three minutes to firing point, Captain!" came the voice of the torpedo officer.

"Hang on to 'em for three minutes, boys!" the captain shouted. "I always said we oughtta have a chaplain aboard this ship!"

Einar, as quartermaster with the rough log long forgotten, had little to do. He envied the man at the wheel, the men at the guns. He could only pray, hold back his fear, make himself stand still and remember. Try to remember what he could of his life, of times gone by. Of being a carefree kid in high school, of boot camp, of friends, of growing up. And the events of the last year that had burned boyhood out of him, showing what could lie beneath the surface of a young man's sunny world. Puget Sound bright in the sun, the snowy Olympics marching in procession on the western horizon and Mount Rainier like a vast white cone-shaped cloud floating in the southern sky. And. . . .

"Thirty seconds, sir! Steady on firing course, please!"

"Very well. Steady on firing course, Helmsman!"

Twenty-five seconds now. A shell screamed so close overhead that Einar staggered. The *Johnston* lined out.

"Twenty seconds."

Einar was holding his breath, counting. How could seconds be so long? Now all was one crescendo of noise, but an icy inner silence held Einar and he could hear the count. Who counted? Captain? Himself? God?

"Ten seconds."

God be with us, God be with us, hold her straight, Helmsman.

"Five." Shell splashes. The sun dazzling in Einar's eyes. "Four." Every man on the bridge was statue still. "Three." The skipper was staring over at the cruisers, shoulders square. "Two." This was all he could. . . . "One." Einar gripped the screen hard.

"Fire!"

The destroyer lurched as thirty thousand pounds of torpedo, ten long, gleaming extensions of man's destructive genius, slid out of the nests of tubes, splashing into the water.

"Torpedoes away!"

"Hard right rudder! Flank speed!"

"Fish running hot, straight and normal, Sir!"

They had done it, they had done it! Now the *Johnston* had made a 180-degree turn, racing back as she had come. Sun and sky vanished as she plunged into her own smokescreen. Everybody on the bridge was shouting now, jumping, unable to hold still. Einar felt that his face was wet and that he was yelling with the rest.

Somebody was counting again over the intercom. Torpedo officer.

"One minute to impact time." Had that much time passed? The smoke was thinning; in a moment the *Johnston* would be out of its protection and in the open again.

"Five seconds! Five seconds, Skipper!"

Quiet now. Black above changing to gray. Open ocean show-ing through rifts.

"Mark!"

Through the distance came hollow, resounding explosions, continuing, and Einar could feel the *Johnston* quiver a moment later as underwater waves reached her.

"Right on!" Commander Evans shouted. "We made a hit, boys! More than one!"

Then the destroyer slashed out of the smoke into the open. Einar saw the leading cruiser of the column sheering to one side, a mass of flame and smoke pouring from her amidships! She was dropping out of formation, falling back, burning. He saw another explosion as he watched—ready ammunition, probably. He was shouting, everybody was shouting! Sun was on his face, the captain's exultant face was shouting at him, blue sky. . . . Planes were flashing silver in the sky above the cruisers; bombs sent up pillars of water astern of the three remaining cruisers, which were maneuvering violently, still firing. Fine rain was blowing into Einar's face though the sun was still shining. He could see a rain squall to windward, moving down toward them, its rain blowing ahead of it.

The sky fell on the *Johnston*. Einar was lost in a rending, shaking mist of red and black, rushing air, screams, roars. The destroyer beneath him was tossed and smashed like a roughly thrown toy ship.

Blackness cleared away, but Einar saw the scene through a moving latticework of red stripes. They faded, and he smelled smoke, oil, a sweet stinking odor of burning flesh and, oddly, coffee. He looked about him at disaster.

Again the sky fell, and something came whirling down, smashed the director above and fell onto the signal bridge. Einar looked up, still staggering, and saw that the big SC radar antenna, the whirling bedspring, had been shot from the mast to fall on the ship. Someone was screaming aft; he was later to learn that the falling antenna had killed three men, some not instantly. The destroyer was wallowing, the whine and hum of engines stilled.

"I can't steer her, sir, I can't steer her!" the helmsman shouted from his post. "Lost all steering, sir!"

Einar saw a form on the deck before him. It was naked to the waist, now it was moving, rolling over, coming to its feet. He saw the powder-blackened face. The skipper! Einar leaped forward to help this man he so vastly admired.

"What the devil?" Commander Evans muttered. His hairy torso was unmarked, except by black areas of burned powder, but his clothes had been blown off above the waist. Einar stared. The captain rubbed his left hand across his face.

"Captain Evans!" Einar gasped. "Your hand!"

"What's wrong with my hand?" the skipper asked, the hand across his chest, blood dripping from it.

"You've lost two fingers, sir!"

"Oh? Fingers. Well, by the Lord, so I have. No matter. If that's the worst that happens to me. . . . What have we got left, Andersen? Any reports coming through?"

Expecting immediate death, Einar rallied and turned to the

intercom. In that moment, the bright blue sky darkened, gray clouds and mist swirled around the *Johnston* and the rain squall roared down. Cool rain poured down his body, over his face, dripping from his hair. It refreshed him, and the swirling inner mists faded away. Damage reports came in: all gun stations were operable, but the three guns aft were on partial local control, no longer directed and fired by radar. The gyros were gone. The after-fire room and engine room were totally knocked out—maximum speed henceforth would be seventeen knots. Dead, dying and wounded men sprinkled the ship. No one knew how many. The screaming had stopped on the signal bridge. The captain was pale, but contained. Einar managed to get the pharmacist's mate on the sick bay phone and had him come up on the bridge.

"Take care of the people that are really hurt," Commander Evans snapped. "Nothing wrong with me."

Einar shook his head at the pharmacist's mate; he managed to persuade the skipper to let the man bandage the hand and stop the bleeding.

"Hot fragments, Captain," the pharmacist's mate said, as he wrapped the bandage rapidly around the captain's hand. "They cauterized the stumps as they went through—red hot, I guess. Anyway, not much bleeding."

"Good. Snap it up, man. I got things to do!" The skipper looked over at Einar. "Andersen, tell Mr. Hagen to continue firing as soon as he can see the enemy. Use local control where he has to."

Einar passed the message on. The pharmacist's mate finished with Commander Evans and vanished. The commander left the bridge for twenty seconds, and returned wearing another freshly pressed khaki shirt and gold-trimmed cap. By that time, with the exec handling things aft, steering had been shifted to the after-steering room, with the JV phone circuit linked in with the bridge for steering orders. All guns were ready to resume firing. The radar stable element was back in operation, and the *Johnston* was moving at the seventeen knots she could still accomplish. The rain squall was still gray and wet about them, and Einar could not help hoping it would last forever. Not Commander Evans.

"How the devil can we get out of this! The battle is going on, and we can't see it. Must be something we can do to help!"

The *Johnston* had been badly mauled. She had been hit by three fourteen-inch battleship shells, and seconds later by three six-inch shells from a cruiser salvo. The combination should have finished her; but the battleships were firing armor-piercing shells, and they plunged clear through the destroyer without exploding. The cruiser shells did explode, and their fragments caused many casualities and much damage. For a space of perhaps ten minutes the rain squall sheltered the *Johnston,* and repairs were made that placed her back in operating condition, though with reduced speed and less effective fire control. She had hit the Japanese cruiser, *Kumano* with at least one, possibly two, torpedoes, knocking her out of the fight. But this was not the end of the *Johnston*'s service in this battle.

The six carriers, still unhurt, were racing at their best speed in a curving track that would head them toward whatever help might be available. Every plane they could launch was in the air, striking at the enemy, pestering the enemy when bombs, torpedoes and even machine-gun bullets were expended. The *Johnston,* on the side of the ships closest the enemy, had already attacked the column of heavy cruisers that had been pulling up to port of the carriers. Now the other two destroyers of the screen, *Hoel* and *Heerman,* cut through the American formation and fanned out to take a whack at the battleships that were coming up astern. They were accompanied by the destroyer escort *Roberts.* As Commander Evans on the crippled *Johnston* saw the three vessels bearing toward the enemy, he roared: "We'll go in with the destroyers and provide fire support!"

"Aye aye, sir," the executive officer answered. And the *Johnston* fell in behind the other attackers, though unable to keep up with them.

The weapon that made these destroyer and destroyer escort attacks worthy of enemy notice was, of course, the torpedo. The Japanese knew that any of their heavy vessels that caught as many as two torpedoes would almost certainly be sunk, either this day or the next, since reduced speed and maneuverability would make them vulnerable to air or submarine attack.

The *Hoel* was the screen flagship, and she took aim at the

Japanese battleship *Kongo*, which was astern of the carriers and rapidly gaining. The battleship was 18,000 yards away, ten miles. The crew of the *Hoel* may have gulped a little at this full daylight charge against a vessel thirty times her strength, but there is no record of it. The *Hoel* went in straight for the enemy, apparently not in the least concerned for her own survival. And it was this attitude on the part of the American forces engaged on this smoky, rain-streaked day off Samar that in the end won them relative safety.

Moving in alone at full speed, *Roberts* having been left behind and *Heerman* not yet joined up, the *Hoel* was the object of widespread enemy fire from cruisers and battleships. It was like charging through a forest of shell spouts. At twenty-five minutes after seven—so rapidly had this battle moved since the enemy sighting at 0647—she received a hit on the bridge that knocked out all voice radio communication equipment and killed or wounded several men. Two minutes later, when only nine thousand yards (five miles) from *Kongo*, the *Hoel* launched five torpedoes at the battleship. Before the torpedoes could reach the area of their targets, the *Hoel* caught it. Numerous shell hits knocked out the after-engine room and fire room, demolished three of her five guns and the port engine and jammed steering at hard right. Men sweated to shift steering to manual aft, but in the meantime the destroyer was heading straight for the battleship she had tried hard to torpedo. *Kongo*'s report later stated that she narrowly avoided four torpedoes as a result of this attack. The distraction of the destroyer attack, plus the time lost avoiding torpedoes, gave the desperate American carriers another four or five thousand yards of space and relieved them of the battleship column fire for several crucial moments.

The *Hoel* wasn't done yet. Her course away from the battleships brought her in on a second column of cruisers. At six thousand yards, the destroyer managed to get off five more torpedoes at the leading cruiser, *Haguro*. Though the Japanese later reported that no hits were made, the crew of the *Hoel* saw several great geysers of water rise alongside the enemy vessel; they were sure that they had hit her, though she continued on in the formation.

The *Johnston* was running in and out of smoke clouds and rain squalls ten thousand yards from the enemy battleships, her five guns pouring out five-inch shells as fast as possible, with three of them on local control. She drew enemy fire as well, and Captain Evans was satisfied. He knew that five-inch shells could inflict no serious damage on battleships, but at least he was diverting some fire power from *Hoel* and *Heerman*.

Heerman came roaring through the American formation, ready to join the attack. Her skipper, Commander Hathaway, later reported that visibility varied from minute to minute from one hundred yards to twenty-five thousand yards. The great masses of black smoke emitted by the American ships hung low over the water, mixing with rain squalls and mist patches to make the day a very confusing one for anyone trying to follow the action visually. So bad was visibility that *Heerman* nearly ran down *Roberts,* then later had to back full to avoid running up *Hoel's* battered stern. At 0744 she launched five torpedoes at *Haguro,* a favorite target. Again the Jap cruiser was forced into wild evasive action.

Five torpedoes had left the tubes of the *Heerman* when her gunnery officer, Lieutenant Meadors, spotted the two approaching battleship divisions less than five miles away. The remaining five torpedoes were immediately redesignated for battleship duty. Commander Hathaway, the skipper, changed course to 270 degrees to get himself in a better position for firing. At the same time he directed his five-inch guns to open fire on the *Kongo.* As he did so, the splashes from Japanese battleships' main batteries began spacing themselves closer and closer to the destroyer. The *Heerman,* finding herself in a good bow shot position on the second Japanese battleship, the *Haruna,* launched the rest of her torpedoes at her and began retiring, chasing salvos.

Torpedoes from several American ships were streaking their way toward the battleships. The greatest of them all, *Yamamoto,* had four torpedoes chasing her astern, two to port, two to starboard. She had changed course to north to avoid an earlier spread; now, unable to turn again, she streaked north and away from the fight, torpedoes astern on either side. She had to continue so for over ten minutes, until the torpedoes expended their fuel and sank. By that time the big battleship was nearly out of the fight, since the carriers had been moving at full speed to the south during the same interval.

So the swirling battle continued. As yet no American ship had been sunk, though the two destroyers *Johnston* and *Hoel* were severely crippled. And ship after ship of the enemy fleet had dropped behind. Smoke rose from fires on several of them, but the day's end was far off.

EIGHT

DEATH OF WARRIORS

TOM BELLIDO, standing by the ready gun of the *Gambier Bay,* found himself crying as he looked out over the smoke-shrouded, rain-streaked sea. He was ashamed. He tried to hide it.

Japanese cruisers had been pouring up on the port beam, their guns already firing at the carriers. Astern, four Jap battleships had been surging nearer, the monstrous spouts of their fourteen-, sixteen- and eighteen-inch guns marching closer and closer. Now they sailed in disarray; cruisers were heading every way, one battleship was moving off to the north and the others, all of them, had stopped firing at the carriers.

Why? Because the destroyers of the screen, three small vessels outclassed in guns, armor and size, had charged in against an overwhelming enemy. Tom had heard of sacrifice and selflessness, but they had been empty words for him, totally apart from everyday life. Now he stood on the fantail of the *Gambier Bay* seeing ordinary people, some of whom he knew very well indeed, interposing themselves between the carriers and the rapidly approaching enemy. Columns of cruisers, divisions of battleships, and between them and their prey were only the long, thin destroyers.

Tom saw these vessels, which he recognized from the many days of common action and purpose, place their battered hulls between the powerful enemy and the carriers. The *Johnston,* with Einar Andersen aboard, mast gone, bridge a travesty of the normal destroyer bridge; the *Heerman,* with wreckage obvious all over her long length. But still they put themselves between the carriers and death! Tom stood with his cheeks wet, looking at them.

Ashamed of himself for this display of feelings, he looked about his gun crew and saw the screwed up faces, the wet cheeks, the indications that these ordinary American men recognized that they were objects of selfless sacrifice. Tom knew, as they did, that manhood required of them an acknowledgement of the sacrifice, this acknowledgement being a total disregard of their own lives if the fleet, the force, the cause, might thereby live.

The Japanese cruisers pulling up on the port side were coming close. Tom heard the admiral's order from the PA

132

system, which someone on the bridge had hooked up to TBS. "Open fire with the peashooters when the range is clear." The range was clear from *Gambier Bay* to the Japanese cruiser column. Tom coached pointer and trainer onto the leading cruiser. The gun crashed, recoiled and paused, breech open, panting white cordite smoke, for the next round, which the loaders slammed in at once. Tom fired again. As fast as the crew could load, the one gun on the stern of the *Gambier Bay* hurled out the only defiance to the enemy that she could make, except for her planes, which now had shot almost all bullets, dropped all bombs and splashed all torpedoes into the blue sea. On this course returning planes would have to land nearly downwind in order to rearm and refuel. Such a landing on any carrier was dangerous, since it sharply increased speed relative to the deck; and on a small escort carrier the landing was almost suicidal. Most of the planes headed off to the southwest to land on other disengaged carriers of Taffy Two, or even on fields ashore which were now just becoming operational, with Japanese troops still fighting stubbornly on their edges.

These planes were replaced by others, by all planes in the area that could fly. Coached on the target by Commander Fowler, air group commander on the *Kitkun Bay,* who spent nearly eight hours in the air over the targets, they began to make coordinated attacks. They were bothering the enemy immensely and inflicting damage on him.

But all that *Gambier Bay* could do was to make all possible speed and smoke and keep popping away at battleships and cruisers with the "peashooter." Tom Bellido fell into a steady rhythm of effort that somehow fitted itself to his stocky body and cheerful mind. The gun was on local control; the *Gambier Bay* had no fire control radar and director for the handling of one gun. Tom decided that mere rate of fire, noise, smoke and flame was not the object, so he had the pointer and trainer sight the gun after every shot, slowing the rate of fire. He sent a shell out every ten seconds, and every shot was aimed. With this constant, careful activity demanding his attention, he lost his fears. He became cheerful again, roaring out his commands, shouting encouragement, even laughing at the messenger's word to the skipper, carried by PA all over the ship. "Destroyers report all torpedoes expended, sir. Say, things are getting a little bit tense, aren't they? Sir?"

"Tense!" Tom howled. "Any tenser and it'll be past tense!"

"For Pete's sake, Bellido! Think you're back in English class?"

"Braaang!"

"Hey, Tom, we hit that cruiser! I saw the explosion!"

"Well, here's another one! Come on loaders, are you asleep? Jake, are you on? Bill?"

The pointer, on, pressed the firing key. "Brraanngg!"

So it went, through the passing minutes, with heavy shell fire coming closer again now that the destroyers had shot their torpedoes.

"Tom!" called the pointed. "Look out there! The destroyer escorts are making a run! A torpedo run. Oh, my God! Look at them go in!"

A destroyer escort is a small, slower, weaker edition of a

destroyer, designed largely for anti-submarine work. Crew, battery and torpedo supply are about half that of a destroyer. It was in total desperation that the admiral in command sent these small patrol vessels against Japanese major warships. But they bored in at the command, mostly individually.

Tom had learned to recognize these smaller vessels during the months of operations, and he saw them now as old friends. As gun captain, he had only to open the breech, press the air key, insert primers and give the word "ready." He therefore had time to keep an eye on the destroyer escorts as they made their try.

The *Raymond* went after the cruisers all alone, for *Roberts* already had launched her fish in conjunction with the earlier destroyer attack. The *Raymond* turned toward *Haguro,* for she was somewhat on that cruiser's bow and might be able to achieve a possible target angle. *Haguro* spotted the little ship coming at her and opened fire with her eight-inch main batteries. The first salvo bunched a dozen spouts two hundred yards astern of the DE. Tom's heart stopped beating as he watched; it looked as though the DE were hit, but she came on bravely. Another sacrifice, Tom knew, and he directed his pointer and trainer to shift fire to *Haguro.* Maybe they could help a little! The first shot missed, but the second and third exploded among the cruiser's forward turrets. They would not pierce the armored turrets, but surely they caused some damage. Tom prayed and kept on firing. He saw the thin white streaks of torpedo tracks pass the *Raymond,* and saw her violent evasive action. From time to time the DE would be quite lost to view in the forest of shell spouts rising about her.

"They'll get her sure, oh Lord, they'll get her sure!" Bill kept shouting. "Oh Lord, they got her—no they didn't, still going! How far in is she going? What are they going to do, ram?"

The DE was only about three miles from the cruisers, a distance that could be covered in less than five minutes at the two vessels' combined speed. Tom began to fear that the DE's bridge had been wiped out so that she was no longer under command. Then he saw the splashes of her launched torpedoes, and immediately the plucky little ship turned away. The *Haguro* was turning hard, then turning in the other direction, reversing her course. The cruiser column blurred, split up, fell back somewhat. Tom watched and prayed to see the tall towers of torpedo hits, but none came. He let his breath out and turned back to his gun. For a moment he was totally busy; when he could look back at the scene it was to see another DE, the *Dennis,* fish-tailing wildly among shell spouts, her five-inch guns blazing. He saw also the splash of her launched torpedoes, and she too turned and fled toward the carriers, having delayed and annoyed the enemy. *Johnston* was tagging behind *Dennis,* losing ground at her battered top speed of seventeen knots. All of *Johnston*'s guns were blazing, concentrating on the enemy cruisers.

"Tom, for the Lord's sake! What time is it?" Jake groaned. "Oughtn't it to be about sunset?"

"I know how you feel—Stand by!—but it's twenty minutes after eight. Fire!"

Another shot, another in the long series of hopeless, useless firings which, even if they hit, could not stop the enemy. Was it possible, really possible, that only an hour and a half had elapsed since this fight started? Tom couldn't believe it, but his watch told him it was true. Ahead, beyond the leading carriers, was only empty sea, and behind, to either side, still rushed pursuing death.

At 0826, Admiral Sprague ordered the destroyer escorts to put themselves between the again-gaining cruisers and the carriers. Tom, hearing the order as well, could hardly bear seeing them do so, but they closed in, almost like rowboats against the heavy cruisers. Again, the cruiser fire was shifted from the carriers to the DE's, which now had to take up the tasks of the destroyers of the screen, all falling behind because of battle damage.

The leading Jap cruiser, *Tone,* was now on the carriers' port beam, and she took the DE's under fire. *Butler,* trying vainly to get far ahead enough of the cruiser to fire her three torpedoes, the only ones left in the American screen, was firing her five-inch at the enemy. *Dennis, Roberts* and *Raymond* were with her, their guns barking steadily as they swirled, zigzagged and dashed among shell spouts. The American vessels were miraculously lucky this day, but now luck ran out for the DE's. All three were hit; Tom, watching, firing, weeping, saw *Dennis* hit and battered, black smoke rising, fire showing, guns silent, limp back into smoke made by her sister ships. *Butler* fell away, making all speed in toward the carriers. *Roberts* began to explode, bow to stern, as shells hit. She lost way, still being pounded by a vengeful enemy. Explosions ran fore and aft; her mast went down. She heeled over, further and further, dropping rapidly astern. The last Tom saw of her she was wreathed in smoke, flame spouting from her bridge, and small figures were working around rafts and dropping overboard. Then she vanished, soon to go down, surrounded by Japanese ships which never ceased to fire on her.

"Poor birds!" Tom said. Then the first shell hit *Gambier Bay*. It was on the flight deck forward, but even so Tom could feel the ship leap and vibrate under the heavy shock. He had been expecting this for a long time, but when it happened the impact was bitter. The feeling of invulnerability was lost; the original conviction of doom, which the brave actions of the screen had to some degree erased, came back redoubled.

"Keep firing!" he shouted. "Shellmen!"

Three shells in succession hit *Gambier Bay,* one of the two carriers deprived of smokescreen by the losses in the DE's and destroyers. Fire roared redly forward on the hanger deck; Tom, as the gun reloaded, could hear men screaming in utter agony, and his flesh crawled. The carrier, a large vessel by most maritime standards, was dancing and twisting like a chip in a rapids. More hits, more red blaze, heavy vibration, a rocking, swelling motion that seemed to rock more and more to the port side. The brave, strong vibration of her engines slowed and became ragged. Smoke blew over the gun crew, and Tom could smell burning oil and the fumes of raw gaso-

line, then of chemical foam. He fired on; there was nothing
else to do. He left the gun long enough to look at the other
carriers and found that they were drawing away. *Gambier Bay*
was still struggling onward, but he knew only too well that
she was being left behind, abandoned. Japanese cruisers were
even with her now, firing into her; the battleships were only
a few thousand yards away. They all were shooting at the
American carrier.

Abandoned? Not entirely. Between himself and the column
of cruisers Tom saw the battered misshapen form of the *Hoel*
interpose herself. Lost in the forest of shell splashes, she twisted,
turned, roared forward, stopped, and her guns kept firing on
the enemy. But they found her range. The *Johnston* too was
coming by, her guns blazing at the cruisers. *Heerman,* in
better shape than the other two, was circling back from ahead,
she too coming back to try to aid *Gambier Bay,* now shuddering and burning under hit after hit, down to eleven knots,
slowing, listing to port.

Tom was watching when several heavy shells caught *Hoel;*
she wracked, burst, leaped. Black smoke rose from her, from
fires and the smoke of her own smoke-making, caught up with
her now that she was finally halted. She went dead in the
water and began to settle astern. A terrible fire roared up from
her amidships. Tom's gun fired; he opened the breech and
watched the long shell slide in. He closed the breech, inserted
the primer, felt and heard the gun buck and recoil, opened
the breech again. More hits on *Hoel.* Tom shouted something,
he didn't know what.

At 0855, just five minutes before nine o'clock, the *Hoel* listed more and more, still being hit, and fell over on her side. She wallowed and went down by the stern, with shells still landing on her floating bow and among the life rafts and swimmers. Then she was gone, the white water boiling about the spot where she had been.

"They did it for us, boys!" Tom shouted to his crew, which was beginning to fall away as the hot breath of fire came blowing to them from the blazing hangar deck and the *Gambier Bay* slowed still more. "Get back here; come on—load. Shellman!"

"No more shells, Tom!"

"Where are the passers? Fighting fires? Okay, I'll get some. Bill, Jake, all you guys come on! We can't stop fighting now!"

They went with him, and he ducked below into the hot, smoke-filled passage to the shell magazine directly below the gun.

So long, it seemed to Einar, had he stood on this wrecked and distorted bridge that he had forgotten what it had looked like only a hour or so ago. Fire had scarred it; the windscreen was ripped and torn, and all glass was gone from the pilot house ports, except for jagged pieces and shreds. The director above was blackened and torn, but still operating. The JV phone talker was standing by the captain, face tired but intent, as he passed Commander Evans' steering orders back to after-steering. Over all hung the smell of cordite, gun powder, burned paint, burned rubber and smoke, cleared out by the wind part of the time, at others reeking close again. All the guns were banging away, first at this target, now at that. Einar had lost count of the numbers of times shell spouts had dumped water on the bridge.

Commander Evans' new khaki shirt was wet and limp, his hat was cocked at a jaunty angle and the bandage around his head was wet and spotted red. He was smoking a cigar and holding the seven-fifty binoculars with his right hand.

"Bridge, this is the gunnery officer!"

The skipper stepped to the intercom.

"Go ahead, Guns."

"Five hundred rounds five-inch shells expended, sir. We're going into reserve magazines. Another forty-five minutes of this and we'll be out of shells."

"Very well. Bob, I wouldn't worry too much about running out—of shells, that is."

"I know what you mean, Skipper."

The skipper turned to Einar and smiled grimly at him. "Too bad about *Hoel*, eh, Einar? We've steamed a lot of miles with her. She's gone down in 4,000 fathoms—24,000 feet of water. She ought to rest easy there."

"Yes, sir. I hope so."

"*Gambier Bay*'s in a bad way, now. Well, we'll stay with her. It's a long morning, isn't it, son?"

Einar could only nod. The morning seemed to him already to have been longer than all of his past life. But he expected his future to end before the morning did, so it was just as well that it seemed to last a long time.

Heerman had been mighty lucky; indeed, all the vessels in

the force had been under such intensive fire that it seemed perfectly natural to all hands to be surrounded by shell spouts. Now Einar saw a salvo hit the other destroyer.

"Hang on, Einar!" Commander Evans said calmly. "Is she coming out, or is she going to stay in there like the *Hoel?* Any ship that loses way today is done for! Come on, *Heerman!*"

Heerman came on; she stirred, then surged forward and out of the smoke. She was down by the bow; Einar saw that her catted anchors were dragging their flukes in the water, so low was she, but the big bow wave arose as she picked up speed, the stern settled and the bow lifted a little. Then *Heerman* opened fire with four guns and moved away with undiminished speed.

As he had got used to the constant roar, rumble and clang of gunfire, Einar had also become so attuned to the constant diminuendo-crescendo wail and scream of aircraft engines that he hardly noticed them. Now he realized anew that the air above all the Japanese ships was flecked with the silver specks of planes, the water torn with bomb explosions. The cruiser that had led the enemy column so long was turning away, falling back, great clouds of smoke rising from her decks, bomb splashes making a wreath around her. More planes, more bombs. Another cruiser was spouting black smoke and red flame, fading away, making evasive course turns, thrusting her sharp and tormented bow away from the fugitive carriers.

"Einar," said Commander Evans, calmly. "If we stay lucky another hour, we're going to win this one yet."

"Yes, sir." Einar, the vast fire-speckled, smoke-blackened scene before him, was unable yet to hope, but he knew that this was a man he would follow to the end. If the skipper said so, then, by the Lord, it was so.

"Oh oh," Commander Evans said, suddenly, above the roar of battle. "I've been expecting this. Four Jap destroyers and a light cruiser heading for the carriers—torpedo attack!"

Einar stared at the enemy ships. They were about five miles away, knifing rapidly through the waves, heading for the carriers.

"We'll take 'em on!" Commander Evans said, briskly. "Guns! Open fire on that cruiser."

All of *Johnston* guns were unmasked by the relative courses of the vessels, and once more the destroyer began heavy and sustained salvo fire. Einar saw hits on the enemy cruiser, the flash of bright, white flame, then smoke, then red flame and smoke, all vanishing. *Johnston* was under fire too; time after time Einar felt the jar and shudder that told of a hit, mostly aft, and heard the explosion with ears deafened by hours of such noise. Each time the *Johnston* moved heavily in protest. There was little screaming on the *Johnston,* but a man suddenly hit, not knowing what he himself was doing, might in the first shock cry out. They hushed quickly. All wounded were carried below at once, to the sick bay until it overflowed, then into the wardroom.

Now the range was barely three miles; the fast Japanese cruiser and the four destroyers were devouring the space between them and the *Johnston* at an astonishing rate. Einar no longer worried about his own safety. He was as much a part of the *Johnston* as her engines, propellers, guns, hull—or her captain. The captain's spirit animated the entire ship; resolution and courage making steel, machinery, fuel, guns and men act as his brain demanded. They were all one—ship, captain, men.

"Look at that!" Evans yelled suddenly. "She's turning away!" Hit twelve times by the destroyer's fire, the Japanese cruiser turned away to unmask the destroyer torpedo batteries. It was too early for a torpedo attack; the carriers were still twelve thousand yards away and making seventeen or eighteen knots. Torpedoes fired from this position would have little chance of making a hit on a carrier.

"Take on that first destroyer!" Commander Evans shouted, his round, dark face alight.

Einar relayed this message to Lieutenant Hagen, the gunnery officer.

"Tell the skipper we'll pulverize 'em!" the voice came back. "Having just licked a little cruiser, a mere destroyer is nothing for G.Q. Johnny."

"Hits!" Commander Evans said, a moment later. "See those hits on that destroyer? Lee, see 'em?"

"I sure do, Captain!" the lieutenant answered, his voice jubilant. "We're giving 'em hell!"

Their own guns barking back, the Japanese destroyers moved into echelon and fired torpedoes, then retired. Einar watched the vanishing sterns with disbelief. Then he wheeled to watch the American carrier forces, still making best speed and making smoke. He knew it was too soon; the Jap destroyers had fired too soon, and their fish would never catch the carriers now.

He realized, with a touch of quick sadness, that one place was vacant in the carrier formation. He wheeled and looked aft. There was *Gambier Bay,* smoke pulsing up from her and enemy ships around her and firing into her. The still quickly moving shape of the *Heerman* was making smoke around her and firing into the enemy. "Tom Bellido!" Einar thought, now with something of despair. "Hope he gets out of this somehow." But Einar thought, really, that none of them could possibly survive.

"I've seen everything now!" Commander Evans crowed as he strutted across the careening, smoke-veiled bridge.

Einar had to agree. One crippled destroyer breaking up a four-ship attack, forcing it to fire too soon. All right. So they had done it. Now what?

The Japanese destroyers, having fired torpedoes and circling away, now came foaming back in echelon aiming straight for the *Johnston.* As plainly as any human speech, Einar could read in their attitudes and their courses that they were coming to finish off the *Johnston.* Relatively undamaged, the enemy destroyers could make thirty-five knots to *Johnston*'s seventeen. All it required was an organized and continuing attack to sink the American ship. Einar tried to cheer himself. After all, that had been all that was necessary for the Japanese to have destroyed the entire American force. Maybe now these four destroyers would not have the cold and determined resolution to finish off G.Q. Johnny. At least, he could hope so.

Air attacks were at their height. The heavens were streaked with vapor trails, glinting specks, smoke streaks where a rare American plane went down. Over every Japanese ship hovered a swarm of hornets, diving, strafing, torpedoing, all throwing themselves into the fight in the same manner in which the destroyer escorts and destroyers of the screen had placed themselves between the carriers and the enemy. The entire canvas of this battle was blending into a great panorama of confusion, difficult for any man to unravel, doubly so if he was there enmeshed in the emotions that made this battle so unusual a fight. The historian, in the calm of study or office, might be equally confused by the welter of reports, charts, diagrams, stories. All was noise, confusion, bravery, fire, death, total effort. The shrieking day closed around Einar and carried him with it.

Suddenly he realized that the *Johnston* was nearly dead in the water. Shells had crippled the remaining engine room. Other shells were bursting up and down the destroyer's length. He could see the Commander's sorrowful face. Around the *Johnston,* in a remorseless ring, were the four Japanese destroyers, curving at high speed, circling like Indians around a beleaguered wagon train. Their guns were flashing, pouring in shells, pennants and flags were fluttering on their masts as they closed in. Poor old *Johnston,* quivering, slowing, dying. But still three of her guns were firing back, and Einar saw that they were making hits.

"I guess, Einar," Commander Evans said, "that maybe we'd better begin to think about abandoning ship."

"Yes, sir," Einar said.

"But not yet! Tell Guns to get that destroyer in front; I don't like his looks. Come on, *Johnston,* hit them, hit them!"

Smoke crowded in and over them like a pall for a dying warrior.

NINE

THE INCREDIBLE

No QUARTERMASTER'S DUTIES on the *Johnston* now; a quarter-master dealt with winds, weather, navigation, a moving ship. The *Johnston* was only a floating wreck—except for three guns that still fired back. Einar was the captain's aide, ready at his side. The OD was down, dead; the exec was badly wounded and below. Commander Evans seemed invulnerable. Blown from his feet twice more, scraped by falling debris, shirt ripped by shell fragments, he still walked the bridge and decks of his ship.

"Four of 'em," said Commander Evans, gesturing with his

cigar, which was too wet to light. "Four danged destroyers against one. But we're hitting 'em, Einar! There, see that? Oh, boy. Guns, you're doing well today!"

The shell had burst on the forecastle of a circling destroyer, and its forward gun abruptly ceased fire while the vessel sheared away and out of the circle. Commander Evans shouted in delight, and Einar found himself cheering. Then the captain sobered and turned on his heel to look over the ship.

She was a mass of wreckage. Fires burned in several places; number-one turret was demolished; numbers four and five were out of action. Both engine rooms were gone, and the mast was hanging over one side of the bridge. The *Johnston* was done, but still her two guns fired.

"Einar," Commander Evans said, sadly. "The boys have done mighty well."

"*Yes,* sir."

"So have you, son."

"Well, sir, Captain, you've. . . . It's all been you, sir."

"Humph. Well, we've all stuck it out. Now I want to save as many of these men as I can. PA system's gone, isn't it? Sound-powered phones working?"

"Yes, sir."

Another shell crashed aboard, not forty feet from them. Commander Evans staggered, and a look of intense grief crossed his round face.

"Get on that JV sound circuit, Einar, and tell 'em to put all life rafts over the side, and the wounded in 'em. Be sure water's aboard. Then all able-bodied men except the gun crews and ammunition party into the water to look after the rafts, the wounded and themselves."

"Aye aye, sir. How about you, sir?"

"Oh, I'm no suicide type, son. I'll go too, but last. You go with the first group."

Einar shook his head. "I won't do it."

"You won't?" It seemed odd to be holding this discussion with his captain, here with the world falling. More shells hit, and he could feel *Johnston* settling beneath them. The battle raged, but here in its center, as in the eye of a hurricane, a cold calm seemed to exist. Einar shook his head; Commander Evans smiled and held out his right hand.

Einar knew then that the skipper needed him. Even Commander Evans' tough body was beginning to weaken. Only the relentless will and courage of the man kept the shoulders square. It was a proud moment for him when he took the hand of the skipper of the USS *Johnston* in friendship.

"I used to like to read accounts of the old sailing navy's fights," Commander Evans said, quietly. "If a man got in this fix then, he could haul down his flag and surrender and his men would be saved. No more. No gentlemen at sea anymore. Too bad. Even if we hauled down that flag," he indicated the colors flying on a staff at the stern since the mast was crumpled wreckage, "even if we hauled it down, the Japs could continue to fire."

"Yes, sir." Center of a maelstrom, but Einar saw also that the main battle was now far ahead. The *Johnston* was being left behind, as was the *Gambier Bay;* as had been *Roberts* and *Hoel.*

"And it's partly our fault, too, son," Evans said rather sadly. "You've seen enemy survivors shot in the water, haven't you? So've I. Ah well, that's the way it is. Get those boys on the rafts."

Einar passed the word, but was certain it would make no difference. *Johnston* was undergoing an avalanche of shell hits. Her guns ceased firing, knocked out, and smoke, flame and agony took the destroyer. But on the lee side the rafts dropped into the slowly heaving water.

Standing on the crumpled wing of the bridge with the skipper, Einar saw the swathed figures of the wounded being loaded in slings and transferred from the blood- and oil-smeared decks to the rafts that floated alongside. Men in the rafts or swimming in the water received the wounded and placed them on the rafts. Water breakers were passed down. Slowly, with infinite care, the procession of broken men moved down the *Johnston*'s sides into the rafts.

The enemy shell fire went on. Most of the *Johnston*'s length was dead now, machinery hushed, crew gone, guns silenced. The shells tore at the metal. Fires burned higher.

Einar now wore the JV sound-powered phones, for the messenger had been sent below to help take out the wounded. Then he heard Mr. Hagen's voice.

"Bridge, this is Lieutenant Hagen. Please tell the captain that all wounded—repeat, all wounded—are loaded aboard the rafts."

Einar made the report. Commander Evans moved his blackened, infinitely weary face again, looking over his ship.

"Very well," he said quietly. "It's time for us to leave her. Ever hear that sea chanty, Einar? True, now. Abandon ship."

Without haste, the remaining men of the *Johnston* went over the side. Einar stayed by the captain; for a while he was afraid Evans wouldn't leave.

"Okay, Einar. I'm coming. Still skipper, you know, and my men are going to need all the help they can get in the water. Let's go, son."

Amidships, the water was so close that Einar and the captain didn't jump, they simply stepped into it. Each had his kapok life jacket on, his whistle, his flashlight, his shark knife. The water wasn't very cold. As Einar was dragged back up to the surface by his life jacket, he felt refreshed. Even now, the sides of the destroyer seemed to loom high above him. He saw Evans' head bobbing around, next to the steel plates of the *Johnston*'s sides.

"Come on, Skipper!" he called. "We've got to move out."

Evans' eyes opened; he grinned at Einar, nodding, and began to swim. Einar swam beside him, and slowly they moved away from their ship. None too soon; a salvo of Japanese shells hit the destroyer, with one of them raising a spout where they had been swimming only minutes before.

The rafts were a hundred yards away, and it took Einar and the captain some time to reach them. They had just done so when Einar saw a Japanese destroyer come roaring up alongside the *Johnston*. The American vessel was about gone.

More and more she was listing; her lee rail under water, crumpled, twisted mast already pointing downward. On her stern, the American flag still glinted its red, white and blue. Einar felt funny watching it. The enemy destroyer was pumping shells into G.Q. Johnny.

"Can't they stop!" Evans said, almost to himself. "Can't they stop? She's going!"

Indeed she was. As Commander Evans spoke, the Johnny seemed to heave a sigh and rolled over. Her stern lifted, the bow dropped and swiftly, tiredly, she went down in a swirl of white water.

Einar saw the Japanese captain, standing aloof on his bridge in dazzling whites, raise his hand to his cap in the naval salute as the *Johnston* vanished. Maybe that was why tears blurred the scene for Einar Andersen.

Sunlight was dazzling in Tom Bellido's eyes as he came out of the hatchway, struggling to keep the shells he carried from escaping his arms. His back ached from the load, his head ached from noise and explosion and his heart ached from the deaths of friends and the sights he had seen below. Others of his crew followed him out, each dumping his shells into the ready ammunition box, as Tom had done.

"What's the use of this?" Jake panted. "We ain't gonna stop 'em with this gun—this peashooter."

"No," Tom said doggedly, "but we can keep on fighting." Smoke blew over them, and he could feel the low-riding, drunken lurching of the ship under him. He staggered aft to the gun tub, as far aft on the *Gambier Bay* as a man could get. Enemy ships were all around; the *Heerman* was cavorting just two hundred yards from the stern, her guns blasting.

In the distance, a focus of smoke, flame, and circling destroyers, an American ship rolled over and sank, just as Tom looked.

"The *Johnston!*" he said aloud. "Good-by, Einar!"

The world blew apart.

The world was water, and it was making Tom Bellido cough and gasp. His face was sinking in it. Why? He lifted his head. He was sick, he vomited up water, choking, coughing. A wave lifted him, the wave sloshed fuel oil in his face. Smoke blew over him, water washed him, the fuel oil dropped away, and cool air came into his lungs.

"Well, this tears it!" Tom said aloud, his head clearing. "Got knocked into the drink. Will I get picked up? Guess it depends on who wins this fracas."

"Tom, Tom!" It was Jake's voice; Tom turned around in the water and saw Jake only a few feet away. Wordlessly, the two men swam together, and Tom found that a little of the harshness of the situation vanished simply because he had someone with him.

"Okay?" he gasped.

"Reckon so, if I can get rid of the oil. What the heck happened to us?"

"Blown overboard. Well, guess we only beat the rest of the boys a little. Look!"

The *Gambier Bay* was nearly done; anyone could see that.

Her list was plain, black smoke was pouring from her entire length. But she was still moving, trying to follow her sisters, the white suds still rising from her propeller. She was a few hundred yards away and moving further.

"Guess this does us in, Tom," Jake said, faintly. "I think I'll go ahead and drown. No use draggin' it out."

"No. Jake, no! Look over there, look!"

Tom couldn't believe it himself. Pointed straight for them was the knife bow of the *Heerman*. She was surging up on them with guns still firing. A man in the eye of the ship was waving, then pointing at the two men in the water. The bow turned, the long side slid up; Tom was tossed in the surging water. Then a life ring dropped beside him; he seized it, intertwined it, dragged Jake on it and felt himself and Jake pulled through the water at choking speed.

Gasping, hanging on, he realized that it was against all human probability that a destroyer in *Heerman*'s situation should make the effort to save them. But then all men's behavior on this lurid day had already been against all human probability or calculation. He thought, "Lord, I'm glad that everybody's crazy today!"

The destroyer swung toward them, giving them a lee and a slack; the strain lessened and then they were at the ship's sides, where a cargo net trailed in the water from amidships. Four men already were clinging to it just above the water, their arms outstretched. Tom bumped into the metal plates, got a hand on the net and felt strong hands grab his arms and heave. He came from the water, got a foot onto a heavy manila strand

and climbed, helped by the men with him. As the six of them struggled up the side, the *Heerman* speeded up.

Tom gasped, his knees half buckling. "Man, I want to thank you guys! Boy, oh, boy! You're crazy, or your skipper's crazy, but, boy, am I glad of it!"

Jake was cursing, or praying, Tom couldn't tell which, and adding his broken thanks to Tom's. A tall lieutenant (jg) in wet khakis that had a smear of blood across the front grinned at the two men.

"Of course the skipper's nuts to stop for you! But today, aren't we all? Or we wouldn't be here."

Shells rumbled over; shell spouts dropped water across the deck.

"They've put out a lot of fires for us that way," sputtered the lieutenant. "Either of you men wounded? No? Good. Maybe you'd like to join in with that fire party over there. At the moment, they don't have a fire to fight, but they'll soon be busy again. I hate to say it, men, but the chances are you'll be back in the drink before long, so hang on to those life jackets."

"Hang on!" said Jake. "I ain't ever going to take mine off again, not 'til I'm smack in the middle of Kansas! Man! I'd be way down there playing with the sharks and feeding the fish in general if it wasn't for this good old life jacket."

They were welcomed by the fire party, and shortly afterward a mess cook came by with coffee and sandwiches. Tom was surprised to find that he was thirsty and hungry, and nothing had ever tasted as good as that black, thick Navy coffee, and the thick slab of bologna between two thick slabs of bread. He could enjoy it in spite of—maybe because of, he thought crazily—the fact that Japanese cruisers and destroyers were in sight all around them. The enemy dye-colored spouts were rising about the dodging destroyer, which fortunately had retained full speed in spite of her badly damaged bow. Red, yellow, green, they rose like weird abstract designs out of the blue ocean.

Then Tom saw *Gambier Bay* again and he was glad the sandwich was finished, for he was sure he would have been sick otherwise. The carrier, his ship, his home, was now dead in the water. *Heerman* was attracting all the fire she could, but the enemy ships were concentrating now on *Gambier Bay*. She was listing over, totally afire, shell hits racing up and down her with bright flashes, debris flying and dark objects falling. Men were beginning to go over the sides. Jake was beside him, staring, his teeth chattering.

"Man, I'm glad I've had my bath today! Oh, them poor guys! Maybe we can pick 'em up!"

Tom knew that if the *Heerman* stopped long enough to pick up the survivors from *Gambier Bay,* she herself would without doubt be sunk—the only remaining target for several Jap ships. She had snared up Jake and himself without really stopping—probably the brief change in course and speed had even aided her in evading more hits. But to stop for half an hour? He didn't say anything, but he knew that the *Heerman* couldn't stop.

"There she goes!" Jake cried, tears on his face. "She's going!"

Tormented to the last, shells exploding on her sides even

as she rolled over, *Gambier Bay* capsized, wallowed in white foam and went down, leaving a mass of life rafts, floating wreckage and swimming men behind her. The tall jg came by again, obviously from the bridge. "Ski!" he said to the boatswain mate in charge of the fire party. "We've just gotten orders from the admiral to rejoin the formation immediately. The other carriers are getting in a bad way; we can't do anymore here, but the old man says as we go by he wants you to throw some more life rafts and floats down to the men."

"Aye aye," said Ski. "Okay, men, get at it. You'll only have about a minute."

Sick at heart, Tom helped release the life rafts, dump over the floater nets, sling in the life rings. One man even stripped off his own life jacket and threw it. Then the *Heerman*, still hounded by shell spouts, opened her throttles full and sped out of the ring of the enemy, aided by an angry flight of Hellcats that had seen the carrier go down and now dived on *Heerman*'s tormenters in a strafing run, each plane's six fifty-caliber machine guns raving and spitting as the planes skimmed the masts of the destroyers and cruisers. There were perhaps thirty of them, and the enemy ships broke into furious evasive action. *Heerman,* all guns firing, broke free and went unpursued across the smoke-dotted sea to where the formation of American carriers, hit, hurt, burning here and there, still moved resolutely toward Leyte Gulf, their single guns still firing.

In the far distance ahead, more carriers were beginning to dot the horizon as the running fight moved in on Taffy Two.

Already Japanese battleship shells were raising their towers of water around the nearest of the next group of carriers. Without hesitation, Taffy Two headed the procession of ships moving toward the southwest and reinforcements.

Tom's head was aching now; he couldn't remember when diabolical tumult, screams, thundering of guns, rumble of shells, rending of metal and deck-shaking impact of his own guns firing had not shaken him, wracked his head. Enough! he thought. Good Lord, enough!

The long, weary battle came to a climax. More planes than ever were battering at the Japanese fleet. Cruiser *Chokai* had gone down, and others had dropped from the formation; all the vessels had received some sort of bomb hits, torpedo hits or shell hits. At these close ranges, even the five-inch guns of the carriers had caused significant damage. And the stubborn American ships, which should long since have been sunk, kept stubbornly on, refusing to give up. The incredible *Heerman,* her bows half caved in, dashed back and forth between battleships and the fleeing carriers. Taffy Two's planes had been in the fight all along; now they were joined by many of those of Taffy One. The Japanese admiral had sighted the American carriers ahead, and he thought hauntedly of the Third Fleet and wondered if he was now going to face that redoubtable and powerful force. The sense of doom he had felt since the battle started reasserted itself, stronger than before. Planes were everywhere, smoke everywhere, blotting out rain squalls and ships, blowing in the wind.

The American aircraft attacked everywhere like furies, never ceasing. The Japanese couldn't tell a plane that had used her bombs and fired her machine-gun ammunition from one that was fully armed, and each screaming plane had to be repelled. Men were losing their self-control and their will to fight. It was hard to keep open bridges and unsheltered AA guns manned, for the decks of all the Japanese ships were littered with white-clad bodies that no one had had time to remove.

Admiral Sprague was on his bridge, watching Japanese torpedoes from cruisers and destroyers passing astern of his ship. Then he heard a signalman yell, "Dag nabbit, boys! They're getting away!" Incredulously, he watched the entire Japanese fleet turn away, reverse course! Only two cruisers were left afloat of the four that had been haunting his port beam all morning, and, one after the other, they reversed course and moved astern. He sat down again, dazed, weary and numb, and heard from all over his flag ship the yells and cheers of his jubilant crew, men reprieved from a death they had thought unavoidable.

Tom Bellido couldn't believe it, he just couldn't. In awe-struck silence the men of the *Heerman* stared at the enemy, now rapidly fading back toward the horizon. Guns still roared, but slowly the firing dropped away. Colored shell spouts ceased to search the sea. Men were muttering, crying, then shouting, leaping, flailing each other, stamping the still solid decks.

Einar, in the water, held up by his lifebelt, swam alongside Commander Evans, who was herding the last individual swimmers to life rafts and wreckage. He saw the Japanese forces coming back from the smoke-shrouded, distant horizon whence the low rumble of gunfire and bombs had been pulsing across the water. Planes still pursued them, but even the air attack was slackening off now. The carriers saved, the nearly fuelless, weaponless planes turned and flew for the nearest dry place to land. Some with fuel and bombs still persisted, and Kurita's once mighty Center Force moved away among bomb bursts. The planes kept the ships too busy to shell the floating masses of American men in the water.

Commander Evans said, "They're running. We won. We won!" Then Einar saw the tears on his cheeks, and he knew that his captain was thinking of his ship, his men.

The Japanese turned away. The main part of the battle was won. But to the north another action was flaring. And as the men of Taffy Three rejoiced, a new danger blew closer on the wings of a ghastly wind.

Now, briefly, a strange calm settled over the carriers of Taffy Three. The last fires were put out. No guns fired. Wounded were tended; damage control parties worked feverishly to repair and restore functions. Cooks and bakers went to work. Tired men ate. Screen vessels remaining came alongside the less damaged carriers to refuel and take on more ammunition and supplies. *Heerman* came alongside *Kalinin Bay* to refuel, to transfer those wounded in need of the superior medical facilities of the carrier and to take on five-inch shells. Among the other men riding the breeches buoy over to the large vessel were Tom Bellido and Jake White. Carrier-trained, they would be more useful on another carrier.

Tom was assigned a bunk and locker. He looked at them both, then put his face in his hands as he remembered *Gambier Bay* and his friends.

TEN

DEATH FROM THE SKY

OCTOBER 25, 10:45 A.M. Taffy Three, its ranks thinned by the loss of *Gambier Bay, Johnston, Hoel* and *Roberts,* was patching up damage and recovering the last of its own aircraft. Below decks on the *Kalinin Bay,* Tom Bellido closed the door of his new, empty locker, and thought about finding the ship's store for skivvies, razor and toothbrush. He looked up to see a chief gunner's mate approaching.

"My name's Bryant," the chief said. "You Bellido?"

"That's right."

"Off of the *Gambier Bay?* Well, I'm sorry about your ship. Know how you feel."

"That's okay," Tom said, rather wearily. "You want me?"

"Can you handle a forty-millimeter mount? We lost a mount captain this morning."

"Sure. I can handle it."

"All right, Number Two Mount, port side, forward. I'll take you up there now."

They were walking across the flight deck when somebody shouted. Tom didn't hear very clearly—he was still deaf from the hours at the gun. Bryant whirled and stared. Following his gaze, Tom saw the black, swift shapes of several aircraft diving on the next carrier in the formation, *Kitkun Bay;* engines sounded from other directions as well, and he realized that they were attacking all the carriers. He and Bryant started to sprint toward the gun gallery. Tom was still on the flight deck when he saw the enemy plane dive directly for the carrier's bridge, strafing as it dived. It missed the bridge and crashed into the port catwalk, then catapulted into the sea. From the point of its impact a heavy explosion rose, and Tom winced inwardly. Oh God! Won't it ever end?

Tom hit the saddle of the forty mount; its crew was in place—loaders, shellmen, clip handlers. Tom saw another plane off to port and swung the entire mount toward it. Shell clips rasped home, clicked. Four guns were under Tom's hand, each ready to pour sixty rounds a minute of shells over an inch and a half in diameter. The four together sprayed these powerful shells like a hose spraying water. The *Fanshaw Bay* was on the port side, and Tom saw the silver glint, high, nosing down, sky clear beyond it. Tom caught it in the sight and squeezed the firing button. Then he was caught up in the spaced maniacal pounding of the mount. The sight was good, but tracer was better. Moving the tracer like moving a stream of water, Tom brought the fire onto the plane. Flashes of light pounded its wings; black smoke and flame grew from the fuselage; the plane nosed over and splashed into the water.

The mount's clatter ceased and Tom was able to hear, above the shouts of the crew, the voice of Bryant.

"Aft! Swing aft! They're after *Fanny B!*"

The planes were clearly seen; for a brief instant Tom wondered why there had been no warning by radar or combat air patrol. He couldn't fire at these two, for fear of hitting the *Fanshaw Bay.* No need. One plane exploded in air; the other dived into the sea, heaving up a gout of flame and brief heavy smoke. Two more circling around over *White Plains!* This carrier was close enough so that Tom could fire above her, knowing his shells would pass clear. The sky above *White Plains* was streaked with tracer and the black bursts of heavy shells equipped with proximity fuse. The planes pulled out of their dives, hardly five hundred feet above their target. One was smoking. Tom sprayed the forty-millimeter shells furiously at it; it banked, climbed, and then dived squarely into another carrier, the *St. Lo.*

Tom knew enough of planes and ships to realize what a fearsome projectile an armed plane was when it struck. The plane itself would explode in a great, searing storm of gasoline flame; the bombs would pass on through the flight deck and explode below. Even the engine would smash loose and make itself into a projectile. The havoc could be terrible.

So it was now. Fire bloomed twice masthead high on the *St. Lo,* and a heavy explosion pealed across the water, shaking the *Kalinin Bay.*

"My God!" Bryant exclaimed in shock. "Look at her go up!"

One after another seven bellowing explosions tore *St. Lo* apart. Fires below deck were setting off torpedo warheads, bombs and gasoline. A fire storm raged above the carrier, flame reaching now several hundred feet in the air, while the vessel itself was hidden by smoke.

"She's gone!" Bryant said. "She's gone!"

He was right. Within minutes, the *St. Lo* went down, but the men of the surviving carriers had no time to mourn. The kamikazes, the suicide pilots who made their planes living projectiles at the certain cost of their own lives, came on, frightening in their deadly inhumanity.

The surviving plane of the pair that had tried to hit *White Plains* came doggedly on, circled the entire formation in a storm of AA fire and then started a straight run at *White Plains.* She flew into the combined fire of a score of guns; Tom could see the tracers ripping into her, the explosions at the wing roots and in the fuselage. The plane had nearly reached the *White Plains* when it rolled over and dived, exploding close to the side of the ship, a few feet below the port catwalk.

"They're crazy!" Bryant shouted. "What have they done to themselves! That pilot was hit twenty times, but he kept going in, going in!"

The men were white-faced. They had faced bitter danger

for hours this day with a joking, almost gay, fatalism. Now the short hairs on their necks bristled at the grisly thoughts of the doomed pilots in doomed planes steering straight for them, making no attempt to bomb or torpedo.

"It's like being attacked by dead men!" a clip man said, his face pale. "Chief, you reckon they are dead before they come in?"

"Aw, thunder, Mac. Don't be a jackass! It's just like the banzai attacks ashore. The Dogfaces and the Gyrenes have been handling them for years. That's all they are—banzai attacks. Now that we know, we'll get 'em. See any more planes, anybody?"

No more were in sight, but with sick foreboding the crew gathered up brass, brought up more clips from below and refilled the ready boxes.

"You want me to go on handling the mount, Chief?" Tom asked Bryant.

"You got a plane, didn't you? Sure I want you to take her. My job is to keep 'em all firing. Keep a sharp lookout, everybody. When we see 'em we shoot. No waiting for 'open fire' against these birds."

The men fell silent, looking at each other uneasily. Then all eyes turned to sea and sky. An unnatural silence fell over the whole ship. The sound of an airplane motor made brave men jump, brought a hundred faces turned in its direction. How can they do it? Tom kept thinking. How can they get in those planes, knowing that they will dive them into a ship, if they can! How can they come on, themselves hit, already dying, and make that burning, falling plane go on, flying it with burned hands, faces, feet? A sick horror gripped him. The strain of all that had happened to him was mounting, building.

The respite was short. At 1110 hours, a flight of fifteen Judys was spotted approaching the formation. Only four carriers remained now, and all the surviving vessels in the screen were picking up survivors of the *St. Lo*. This time the Combat Air Patrol spotted the attacking planes. Alerted to the deadliness of this form of attack by the carriers, the American fighters tried to wipe out the enemy. Tom saw smoke trail after trail, saw explosions in midair. But jinking and dodging close to the water or high in the sun, some of the kamikazes got through.

Within yards of the *Kitkun Bay* her attacker lost both wings and fell into the water alongside, fragments killing men and damaging the ship.

Now *Kalinin Bay*, Tom's new ship, was to find what it was like to be attacked by men who, if not already dead, thought of themselves as dead long before the attack started.

Tom saw the plane starting straight in on them. AA fire was rocking the air all about it, but it came on. Tom got his tracers on and, unbelievingly, saw the entire plane burst into repeated explosions from forty-millimeter shells. Still it came on. He saw the canopy fly in fragments, saw the end of the wing drop off, saw the furnace of flame and smoke peeling from the very cockpit itself. Dead man at the controls! Tom thought despairingly, holding the firing triggers down. Noise, fear, death approaching, a terrible crescendo of everything that man or spirit could summon up! Tom fired on.

Breathing heat and flame after it, the plane passed feet above Tom's head. He heard the metallic thunder as it hit the flight deck above him, saw the massive burst of flame move upward to all sides. He had found another target, almost without willing it, and he was shaken by the rhythmic destruction the mount poured forth. This plane, too, grew streamers of flame and smoke, was hit repeatedly and came on. It passed above Tom into the smoke of earlier fires, and he saw it smash into the after-funnel of the carrier, carrying it away, plane and fragments a blazing mass that cleared the ship and fell into the water.

Two more planes dived for *Kalinin Bay*. Both died, missing, and burning briefly and fiercely on the water.

Then quiet. Fire-fighting parties were busy on the flight deck. Fortunately the plane had struck a glancing blow, and the bombs hadn't pierced the strong deck. The flight deck itself was badly damaged, but the fires were out in a few minutes and the carrier could still make full speed. It would be hours, though, before she could handle planes again.

So the kamikazes made their entrance on the scene of World War II in the Pacific. Fortunately they did not appear until late in the war; had this tactic begun two years earlier, it would have been hard to maintain an American fleet in the Pacific. During the last months of the war, thousands of Americans died from these ghastly attackers, and hundred of ships were badly damaged.

Tom Bellido couldn't know this. But as the ship secured from General Quarters and he went below, he knew that he was much older than he had been before, and he knew of more things in the world than he had ever dreamed existed.

Noon came, and the afternoon passed in a frenzy of work and repair. Night came—a cool, sheltering blessing. The battle of Leyte Gulf was over. More cripples would be pursued and sunk during the following day, but the crucial fight itself was finished. The survivors in Taffy Three stumbled like dazed men to their bunks.

Hundreds more were fighting on. The survivors of *Gambier Bay, Hoel, Roberts* and *Johnston* saw the sun set and night climb up from the east, still unrescued, huddled moaning on rafts, swimming with dangling feet in the shark-filled water, hoping, despairing, suffering, dying. They fought on against the immemorial enemy, the sea.

ELEVEN

IN THE DRINK

THE SEA. It surrounded Einar Andersen, engulfed him; it stretched beneath him for nearly five miles, straight down, waiting to see what he would do. Einar had loved it; now he hated it. It was an oil-choked sea, and the stink of oil was in his nose, and the sting of it in his eyes. He shook his head to clear his face and looked around him.

The foam of the sinking *Johnston* still was visible a hundred yards away. To the southwest were the four Japanese destroyers, making speed toward the battle. In that direction were smoke and fire, and the sight and sound of planes diving in the distance. The shapes of enemy battleships flitted in and out of rain squalls, smoke screen and gun smoke. The American carriers were like chips against the horizon.

The battle had left the men of the *Johnston* behind, as well as the men of *Gambier Bay, Hoel* and *Roberts*. The last had gone down only a couple of miles away; the carrier had been six or seven miles distant when she sank, and the *Hoel* was beyond her position.

Now they could only wait. If the Americans won, somebody would be back for them. If not? Einar put that thought from his mind. He swam back toward a nearby life raft. There was the captain, hanging on, talking to Mr. Hagen. He beckoned Einar over.

"We've got to get some organization here," he said briskly. "Einar, I want you to swim around and see that all the rafts are tied together. All the floating wreckage that can carry a man, too. If we stay together, we'll be all right." He looked about him. "This raft is about the center of things; have 'em paddle and swim over this way." The raft was a fairly large rubber one, with a good freeboard. "In the raft! Stick up an oar with a handkerchief or something on it. Tell 'em to come to that, Einar. Bob, you go in the other direction." The captain hesitated. "We want to avoid panic; fear is the worst enemy we have. Okay, boys. Bring 'em in."

To Einar, it seemed as if all the men in the world were swimming about, hanging on to boards, to the sides of life rafts, Carley floats and balsa rafts. All had on life jackets. Einar passed the word, pointing to the upended oar, now visible on a wave crest, now out of sight in a trough. The waves seemed so much larger than they had from the *Johnston*'s decks. The men responded willingly enough; the instinct of men in such a situation is to gather close for support.

It was slow work, but gradually the area of the swimmers diminished. Rafts moved together, floats, balsa rings, life rings, a floating wooden messtable, lifesaving buoys. Finally all were in a roughly circular area about sixty feet across.

"All right, boys!" Commander Evans was standing erect in the raft, making himself heard. "We're all right now. They'll be back for us soon."

"You tell 'em, Skipper!" somebody cried out.

"I'll do that. Now, the first thing is to see that every wounded man is on a raft. If a man is badly wounded, he must be on something that will keep him out of the water. Able-bodied men into the water, now, and we'll see how much room we have."

Einar marveled at the effect of the skipper's calm, confident words and voice. Faces lost their strained looks; somebody laughed.

"Time Jonesy here took a bath!" a man shouted. "But I'll declare, I didn't expect to be in the same bathtub with him."

Several men laughed. Einar relaxed a little. Surging movement was taking place all through the huddled group. Wounded men were hauled from the water to rafts, and unhurt men slipped down into the water. Wounded floating in life-belts were rounded up by swimmers and brought to the

175

center. It became evident that there was room on the rafts and floats for a good many men other than the wounded.

"All right, men, let's count noses. Hold up your hand; if you're beside a wounded man who can't do it, hold up both of yours so that he'll be counted."

The count took some time and wasn't entirely accurate. Including the wounded, there were about 270 men in the group.

"Incredible!" Einar heard Evans say to the Gunnery Officer. "All those hits, and only about fifty killed outright."

"We've got a lot of wounded, sir. A number of them won't live very long without medical help."

"I know—poor guys. Well." Commander Evans got to his feet again, balancing against the sea's surge. "Men, we'll be all right. We made a name for ourselves and for our ship today. Now don't let anything scare you. We've got plenty of forty-fives to scare off sharks with—just hold 'em above the water pointing toward the varmint and shoot. Concussion sends 'em away. Don't lose your heads, and look after each other. We'll pull through. We've got about ninety wounded; they stay on the rafts. The rest of you take an hour on a raft, then an hour in the water. I'll give the signal, or Mr. Hagen here. Now I don't want anybody hollering 'shark!' You'll scare everybody if you do. Just holler 'Ship's Cook!' That'll work just as well, and won't sound as bad."

"Kinda mean to the sharks, ain't it, Cap'n?" a voice twanged from the water.

"If somebody yells 'Ship's Cook,' then I want all of you

to kick and splash all you can. Don't use the forty-fives unless you really see something."

"How about chow down?" another voice called. "Time to hoist the bean rag, Skipper!"

"You want to get cramps, swimming on a full stomach?" somebody else asked, and again there was some fear-erasing laughter. Then Commander Evans sat down in the raft, shoved his feet over the side and slipped into the water.

"Sir!" said Einar. "You're wounded—stay in the raft."

"Me? This mosquito bite? Don't be silly."

"We need you, sir. We need you to hang on to."

"Okay, I'm here."

There was a constant stream of men paddling around the group outside, visiting a friend, searching. Einar saw the torpedoman, a man named O'Gorek, swim up to Mr. Hagen. He said, "Mr. Hagen, we got off all ten of them torpedoes, and they ran straight, hot and normal." He didn't hear Mr. Hagen's reply.

All this had taken time; Einar now was startled to hear the distant explosions coming closer. He looked, and looked again.

"Captain!" he said. "Am I right? Have they . . . ?"

"You are!" Commander Evans shouted. "They've turned away, they're heading north. The aviators are still after 'em, and look at 'em go!"

A cheer ran through the men in the water; even some of the badly wounded raised quavering voices. Miles away, the Japanese fleet moved to the right, northward, retiring. Yelling, exultant men watched them go, and before long all signs of the enemy had vanished into the haze at the horizon. Smoke began to lift from the sea. The sound of gunfire was stilled.

"Now we got it made, men!" Commander Evans called. "We've licked 'em, and that means the boys are on their way back to pick us up right now. We'll make it; all of us will make it."

Time moved faster, with hope spurring it. Now it was noon. Einar's watch, like those of most of the men, was waterproof and shockproof, and it went on ticking as if he were safe back aboard the *Johnston*. The sea remained empty. Not even a plane.

"An hour or so, give or take a little," Commander Evans said. "They'll be here."

When it became Einar's turn to climb out onto a raft, he was reluctant to take it. "None of that, Andersen," the skipper said sharply. "Take your turn. It will help keep you able-bodied, and we'll need all able-bodied men, maybe, before we're out of this."

The drinking water was reserved for the wounded, and no whole man complained. The raft Einar was on held six badly hurt men. They were dazed, but in pain. All had been roughly bandaged and their bandages were wet. The man nearest Einar had lost an arm, and red was soaking slowly through the mass of bandage the pharmacist mate had wrapped around it. Einar tried to help, but at his slightest touch the man groaned with pain. Two others were burned, their faces invisible behind pads of water-soaked gauze. The others lay quietly, groaning a little now and then, one breathing heavily,

178

almost as if snoring. Einar was filled with great compassion for these torn men. One man's hand was dangling over the side of the raft; Einar brought it gently back, and tried to rearrange the men in as comfortable attitudes as possible. The sun was on their faces, and they looked old, old, as if already part way out of this world.

The sun swung down toward the west, and with its visible drop in the sky the hope and courage of the men dropped likewise. The skipper realized it; he swam from raft to raft, joking, encouraging the men. A horrible thought was becoming stronger for Einar. The sky was empty now, and the ocean was empty, at least to the rim of their water-level horizons. Would they—was it possible—that they'd have to spend the night out here?

"Jeez, they better come soon," one of the wounded men whispered. "They won't be able to see us if they don't."

"Sure they will," Einar said soothingly. "We've got Very pistols and flares. They'll see us."

"Bad time. . . ." the boy whispered. "Bad time. . . . It's getting dark, Einar!"

The setting sun shot up great masses of gold, red and lavender light. Clouds all about the horizon glowed threateningly, blood red, black and red, pale gold, green, yellow. Then darkness rushed down.

"Keep closed up, men!" Commander Evans shouted. "Don't anybody drift away. Don't turn on your flashlights unless we hear a ship or a plane."

Each life jacket had attached to it a small light that would shine red and white for a good many hours, to help a man in the dark be seen by rescuers. But the batteries wouldn't last indefinitely. From time to time a quick glimmer of light showed somewhere in the group as a man tried his torch.

The night. The long, long night. The wounded moaned patiently. Einar went back into the water again. Later, he exchanged places with another man on a raft.

Ages went by. Sometimes the curved sweep of phosphorescence showed where a fish passed beneath the swimmers; several times there were cries of "Shark—Ship's Cook!" and several times forty-five automatics barked hollowly, their muzzles only inches from the water. No one was attacked.

More ages. Stars swung. "Why aren't they coming, why aren't they here, oh why, why, why don't they come after us?"

Hours and ages. Swinging stars. A cold dragging from below where a man's helpless feet swung and kicked above five miles of water. What was down there? What was waiting?

Einar didn't understand time, but after that night he knew that it was flexible. One hour does not equal one hour. Not in time. The night was longer than his lifetime.

Darker darkness first. Then, truly seen, not just imagined, one horizon had a steel-gray tinge to it. Rain began and ceased after a hard pelting that filled Einar's mouth a dozen times with sweet water. The gray was stronger; suddenly it was dim daylight, and in the east the sun was a red glow.

"Skipper!" said Einar, swimming around the raft to where Commander Evans had been holding to a line half an hour ago. "Daylight. We made it, sir, we . . ."

Commander Evans wasn't there.

Commander Evans wasn't anywhere in the group. He was gone.

Frantic searching, deadening despair, slow anger, savage, cursing, roaring rage—nothing brought him back. The captain of the *Johnston* was gone.

He wasn't the only one. Three of the six wounded men on Einar's raft were dead. Every raft carried some dead. Men in the water like the captain, feeling the end, had simply disappeared.

Now, Einar thought. Now comes panic, and a terrible mess. The men all knew that the captain was gone. Even the wounded on the rafts knew it, and many of them cried a little. Einar waited for the moment of panic to come, for anger and hopelessness to burst the orderly discipline Evans had imposed.

A cold emptiness grew within him. Not just the cold of water, hunger, thirst, weariness. But the cold of hopelessness, and in instants Einar felt it numb his limbs, slow his lungs, cool his blood and make death seem a next-minute proposition. The captain's gone, his mind said. The ship's gone. You're forgotten. You're . . .

His mind wasn't allowed to finish. He heard a man shout something; he looked up to see Mr. Hagen balancing in the life raft. He called out again for attention.

"All right, men! All right, *Johnstons*. We made it through that night, and they'll pick us up today. We've lost some men, God rest them. I know the service for the burial of the dead at sea. We will bury them now. Then we'll open emergency rations and have something to eat, and a little water. All rafts close in. Raft captains! Bring 'em in. Stay together now."

Commander Evans was gone, but the *Johnston* still had a captain. Before the cold loneliness that each man there had felt at news of Evans' loss could grow to panic, the new captain had taken over. Calmness and authority were in his voice. Life proceeded for the crew of the *Johnston*. Einar, with the rest, felt his hope renewed.

With all reverence possible, they sank the dead into the sea.

Long morning of hope, noon of warmth, then faces and arms tenderized by immersion began to burn. The afternoon. Waning hope. The night again. Despair.

The survivors of the gallant ships of Taffy Three had not been forgotten, but things had gone wrong. From that first day, ships were searching for them. The kamikazes had been attacking over a wide area; new disasters and damaged ships filled men's minds. But the *Johnston,* the *Hoel,* the *Roberts* and the *Gambier Bay* were remembered. A first fatal report had given the positions of the survivors nearly forty miles wrong. The searches had failed. Another report put them as many miles in another direction. No one could explain why. The admirals in command felt frustration settle into cold rage, and more searching forces were ordered out. Finally a task force of eight small vessels were sent to sweep visually the entire area for as long as was necessary to find the abandoned men.

Cruelly, ironically, during that day several American planes had buzzed the floating masses of survivors and had gone on without dropping anything, without making a report. This was never explained. Possibly these aviators were so sure that help was on its way that they hadn't bothered to take any action. At any rate, it happened.

There was more room on the rafts now, with many of the wounded dead and gone. For two hours out of three Einar was on the raft, then back in the water to swim, to patrol, to encourage, to strengthen. Sharks came that night. Forty-fives came into play. Several men vanished, killed by sharks. A chief gunner's mate was bitten twice but each time released. He crawled out on a raft to stay there, one of the wounded. His raft-mates told him he must taste like the devil himself to make a shark spit him out.

Mr. Hagen held them together, but he too was growing gray and distant, like a man moving partly in another world. Einar was acting as his aide. Seeing the sun come up made Einar more cheerful, but Mr. Hagen said to him quietly, "They'd better come today, Einar. I don't think they'll find anybody if they don't."

Einar had wound his watch. It was just 9:25 when he saw to the west a dark spot emerge into the air above the horizon. He studied it vaguely for a moment, then he realized what it was—a ship! A landing craft, or a subchaser—but a ship! His voice was gone, but the croak he forced out brought other eyes around, and seconds later a Very flare went hissing into the morning sky.

Rapidly the thing on the horizon drew closer, and an answering flare made a streak of light against the western sky.

By ten o'clock, all the battle's survivors were aboard a fleet of landing craft and PC's. By ten-thirty they were on their way to Leyte Gulf.

From the *Johnston, Hoel* and *Roberts,* one hundred and sixteen men who had made it safely into the water—including Captain Evans—died during the two days' wait for rescue.

And to Einar Andersen nothing else had ever felt as good as the dry, warm deck beneath his body, and the knowledge that before very long he would stand on land again.

And nothing had ever felt so bad to him as the knowledge that he was leaving behind him his ship—and his captain.

TWELVE

THE AFTERMATH

THE NAVAL BATTLE for Leyte Gulf was over, although men continued to die in the Philippines. The army fought Japanese ground forces on Leyte; the navy countered increasing kamikaze attacks; the airmen strafed and bombed over land and sea. The war went on, but the battle a thousand miles wide was finished.

The Japanese ships had gone down in the Palawan Straits, in the Sibuayan Sea, in Surigao Strait and at sea off Samar and Cape Engenao. In this one great battle Japan had lost three battleships, four carriers, six heavy cruisers, four light cruisers, thirteen destroyers and several hundred planes. Her manpower losses can only be estimated, but they must have amounted to ten or fifteen thousand trained naval personnel.

Of the American fleet one light carrier, two escort carriers, two destroyers, one destroyer escort and one submarine had been sunk. Other vessels had been heavily damaged. One thousand one hundred and thirty officers and men were dead or missing; nine hundred and thirteen had been wounded.

The fight had been a savage one, and the American victory had not been easily won. At several points it had seemed that the Japanese might emerge victorious. But after the defeat at Leyte Gulf, Japan had lost control of the Philippines. This being true, thinking men could foresee the end of the war. The naval victory had cleared the way for victory ashore.

Even more significantly, Leyte Gulf marked the end of the Japanese Navy as a force that could be effective in a major way. There still was a Japanese Fleet with battleships, converted carriers, cruisers and destroyers—but it could no longer seriously threaten any major American task force. American control of the sea stretched almost to the shores of the Japanese Islands themselves. But the road to Japan was long, and the journey would be a terrible one.

For some of the men who had been engaged in the battle there was rest—for a time. Until the next move toward Japan.

It was a lazy afternoon. Palm fronds rustled in the trade wind. The white sand glistened in the sun, stretching down to the water's edge, where men frolicked noisily. Others played softball and volleyball on nearby fields. Many simply lay quietly in the shade of the palm trees or sat and talked—remembering.

In one shady corner of the palm grove, five young men were stretched out on the green grass. The royal palms curved above them; beyond the shade the white-hot sun brought the vast anchorage of Ulithi into clear focus. One of the men, a freckle-faced Irishman, was sitting against a palm looking up at a tall blond man who had been having some difficulty smiling.

"How did you get hold of us all, Einar?" Jerry O'Donnell asked, taking a long drink of his ginger ale.

He didn't really care about the answer; he had just thought that the silence had gone on too long. When people didn't talk, he remembered all too well. The shells, the lights, the hotness, the screams! He remembered how the PT had looked as she slid off the beach and sank. His memory of the battle included darkness and terror. He sometimes thought of the O'Donnell who had been cocky and self-assured—so different then from what he knew himself to be now.

"I ran into Clay the first day I came ashore," Einar explained after a moment. "I knew where the rest of you were, and the Chief Signalman of my destroyer let me use the blinker. So here we are."

"Yeah." Jerry drank again, sighed and stretched out. "Doesn't that dry land feel good under you?"

"Yes!" exclaimed Einar. Jerry looked at him and nodded, not speaking.

Einar felt the tension rise within him. Maybe he had emphasized that "yes" too much, but he couldn't help it. He knew that he would never forget those hours that had stretched into days, the days that had become endless years, when he had hung suspended over a chasm with death rising now here, now there, to take a man from among the survivors of the *Johnston*. And the skipper. Just vanishing like that. Einar knew that he would never stop in life to think, to breathe, without remembering in some deep well within himself the way the skipper had just—vanished. He must have felt himself going, but he hadn't called for help. He had not asked for comfort or encouragement, that man who had comforted and given courage to so many during the desperate hours of the battle.

"Sunshine and fresh air are great too," Clay Harkness added, taking off his shirt. "I think I'll go for a swim."

Sunshine and fresh air. Not a submarine jammed on a reef in the darkness with an enemy destroyer coming close. And not stuffy darkness below the ocean, when enemy depth charges clanged all about. He remembered the sight of that Japanese cruiser flaming, sinking, exploding. He shuddered as he recalled the macabre closeness of the breaking-up noises the vessel had made as she sank.

"Wait until I finish this and I'll go with you," Tom Bellido said.

"We'll all join you." Jerry yawned widely. "Then I think I'll take a nap."

None of them wanted to talk much about the battle. For some reason a constraint had been hanging over them, but it was fading away now. The five of them, not looking so terribly different than they had a little over a year before, started down to the beach. They paused and looked out over the huge circular anchorage. The fleet lay there in rows, an almost unimaginable array of sea power. It was organized, ready, poised to the last ship and the last man.

"I came down to help pick up six new PT's arriving here by tanker," Jerry said. "They want 'em up north pretty bad."

"Another one starting," Einar said softly.

"Yeah." Tom scratched his close-cropped head. "I hope it's not like the last one."

Gambier Bay. Tom recalled his thoughts as he had watched the Japanese forces approaching the dying ship. All the things he had never done and now never would do. How he had never told his parents how much he appreciated their sacrifices. How he had never had a girl, would never have a wife. Then the sick despair when he had come to the surface of the water, the conviction that his life was finished. He stirred uneasily, sickness coming back. He thought that maybe saying these things aloud might help release him from them, but he had no skill with words. He dug up one memory that didn't hurt. He said, "I thought about all of Larry's talk about skiing, and I figured I'd never be able to try it."

"Leyte Gulf." Larry White sounded sad. "The biggest one yet. We were in it, boys. It's a thing we'll never forget." He hesitated and then went on. "They say that all of us fought like heroes—but I didn't feel much like one. I was scared every time our plane took off. I cheered when we made a hit, but I didn't really like to pull the machine-gun triggers when we got close enough to see that the Japs were people too. You don't think about it so much when you're way above them—they look more like ants."

Yes, he had killed men, and he didn't like to think of it that way. Yet, too, he felt a sadness, almost nostalgia, a feeling that something was all over. Would he ever again ride that screaming dive down onto an enemy carrier? Was that over and gone? Didn't he want it to be over and gone? Was he nuts or something?

"Heroes," Clay Harkness said. "I know what you mean. I was plenty scared with my boat on that rock and the destroyer coming. But I guess maybe we all acted more like heroes when the chips were down than we ever thought we could. And now the fleet is ready to go somewhere again, and we'll go with it. Well, that's the way it is, boys."

As they looked out over the ships and the great anchorage, an observer would have decided that they had changed after all. They were older in ways that mere time couldn't measure; their lips were set with a firmness beyond their years, their eyes steady and serious. They were tested, tried, all five of them. And they knew that further testing was to come.

"Two weeks ago," Einar said softly. "That's all it was. And here we are. A lot of good guys weren't so lucky. I told you about the skipper, didn't I?"

"Yes," Jerry said quietly. He knew that this was compassion he felt, an emotion that the old O'Donnell would scarcely have recognized.

They stood together looking out over the fleet. The after-

190

noon sun shone brightly. A white sea bird with black-tipped wings swooped low over the grove and rode into the wind, to the northwest. There lay Japan. There lay the next step on the road.

Then the five navy men smiled at each other and ran shouting down the slope and into the blue water of the Pacific.